God's Wife and the Synonymous X

by
JESSE CHASE

8TH HOUSE PUBLISHING

8ᵗʰ HOUSE PUBLISHING
MONTREAL, CANADA

Copyright © 2017 Jesse Chase

First Edition

All rights reserved under International and Pan-American Copyright Conventions. No part of this book may be reproduced in any form or by any electronic or mechanical means, including information storage and retrieval systems, without permission in writing from the publisher, except by a reviewer, who may quote brief passages in a review.

ISBN 978-1-926716-43-5

Design by 8th House Publishing.
Manufactured in Canada.

Cover Artwork by Michel Honoré Prentice

This is a work of fiction. Names, characters, businesses, places, events and incidents are either the products of the author's imagination or used in a fictitious manner. Any resemblance to actual persons, living or dead, or actual events is purely coincidental.

LIBRARY AND ARCHIVES CANADA CATALOGUING IN PUBLICATION

Chase, Jesse, author
    God's wife and the synonymous X / by Jesse Chase.

ISBN 978-1-926716-43-5 (softcover)

    I. Title.

PS8605.H3866G63 2017   C813'.6   C2017- 02362-4

the four narrators and their exorcist: chuckles the urge; the ruling reason aka logic your majesty aka the dandy; story teller aka gravity; MC fractal usurper; asherah as electromagnetism.

1
thursday: wake up

there was no falling back to sleep. just as the darkness turned to light, just before the multitudes of a single death began to secrete into consciousness, he woke up, in a sweat, on a big dense couch of floral pattern. he looked at the neon numbers of the unused VCR above the television across from where he lay, almost noon. sometimes he would jot down what he could remember from dreams. he could only remember the broken picture frame and the face of the editor. he tried to remember the words, he knew how they were meaningful, but where to find them. the lucidity began to fade as time and space settled. he wiped the sweat from his forehead. the pillow under the back of his neck was damp. then his attention honed onto the bathroom at the other end of the three and a half apartment. the sun was glaring down on him from the window.

the toilet flushed and out walked calvin's grandmother. she looked like she was ready to go out somewhere. wuddup grandma? calvin, she said, i don't know how you sleep so late, why don't you wake up early and find a job? i have a job, i'll be workin more soon. he'd been repeating that for weeks. are you goin out? i'm going downstairs. oh, bingo? yes, yes. are you coming? naw, i'm goin to work. ohhh so you're working today? just goin to pick up my pay. oh calvin, don't go out and spend it all this weekend. huh? he was pretending to be too tired to talk now.

every thursday at lunch was bingo day at the golden isles retirement home. calvin would sometimes join in, when he would win he'd notice a few scowls, others just thought he was such a nice grandson because he was spending time with his grandmother. he'd been living with her for the past month and a half. he wasn't working enough to rent an apartment yet.

 the manager of the building had recently taken note of his more than regular presence in the building and mentioned to his grandmother that she would have to pay more rent if he stayed any longer. it was outrageous. it was family helping family. calvin's grandmother was living off her modest pension. once the gossip got around the building that calvin was in fact living there for free some of the tenants supported cal's grandma. if mrs. edie's sister came to visit from jamaica there would be no way she would have her rent increased.

 grandma got on the phone to call her only son, calvin's father, to call the building manager so he could resolve the problem. you don't need to call him for that. how do you think that makes me look when i see the manager. i'll talk to him myself, i'll take care of the problem, i'll be workin more in a few weeks anyway, i'll be gone, i'll take care of it. calvin would say.

 grandma was goin to be eighty-two this year. she was still full of vigour and would joke around with calvin. sometimes she would stay up and watch a movie with him until one in the morning. she would make constant references to cal and his grandfather, who she divorced nearly 50 years ago. you're all the same, she would say about the kale's. so disorganized, drinkin, never know what you're doing, and when you're doing something it's never that much. granny, einstein slept ten hours a day, so did churchill. you never know. the most important and natural thing to calvin, besides friends and fun, was being productive, cataloguing the gestalt of language in time through waking and dreaming spaces. o.k, well i'm going downstairs, granny said wearily. she actually didn't like most of the other tenants, some she had known since she was a child growing up in little burgundy during the thirties and forties. she walked out the door and calvin fell back to sleep for a little while longer.

☙

he woke up to a text message. camping in chicoutimi this weekend, you down? crazy ass. some of cal's buddies had been leaving town every weekend for the past few weeks, he didn't have a dollar he wanted to spend or a desire to go.

as calvin looked in the fridge for breakfast, finding nothing of interest. he smoked his morning cigarette, shit, showered and shaved, brushed his teeth, the same ol' routine start to the day bullshit, dream resin in his eyes, thoughts were coated by an inescapable tone. a daily universal not far from the suns and the earths, the dust of atoms tinted through what it was like between babylon and zion. the flash and colour of life beyond his grandmother's three and a half apartment door erasing everything that came before it, creating a new tone from body to environment. the tone reflected on the clouds of the sky, in which way the cigarette smoke blew, the refreshment of the shower, in the hue of the bathroom's mirror lights.

backpack, slip shoes on, turn dead bolt, slide/glide/pass/sneak/walk through the door. lock and key. (p)resume. since the building manager started disrupting the relative tranquility of granny's cozy apartment, he began to leave through the back stairwell rather than use the elevator. hopefully they're all playing bingo, he didn't like bumping into the neighbours just as much as his grandmother did.

the sixty-four south passed every sixteen minutes. what time was it exactly? enough time to buy a pack of smokes and a bus ticket? fuck it. he walked into the east indian depanneur. hey man, he knodded to the clerk. grabbed a small fruit punch. hey, can i get a pack of john player standard rolling tobacco and a bus ticket? please? sure man, said the skinny brown guy behind the counter. the two of them, calvin and the store clerk, would have little conversations every once and awhile. they'd cooly shoot the shit or the clerk would talk about the last regular who just walked out of the shop. did he say anything about me?

the clerk was quick, he was in the middle of doing something. he put tobacco and a bus card on the counter. calvin's money was already on the counter, he's got no time to waste, the bus is on its way. is that everything? ya mahn, cheers. ok. nineteen forty. twenty dollars. here you go man. cheers, have a good one. good day my friend.

    calvin rushed out of the door that opened from the right rather than the left and walked past the rest of the strip mall shops. the african beauty salon. the sri lankan-owned dep. he turned the corner to see the bus leaving his stop. fuckin eh. a quick pick up of the receiver from the payphone beside him: thirteen and twenty-one hours. mechanics of time and space, didn't really need to know. automatically reached into his pockets and pulled out a crumpled five dollar bill and two seventy-six in change. that's it? shamone. he drank his juice, rolled a cigarette, smoked it. a few folks at the bus stop. the deaf man's cell phone would always ring till it could ring no more. the strangers that didn't see the pack of tobacco thought it was a joint, thought calvin. which is normal. the city looks, it looks like it thinks. looks like it thinks, thinks like it looks, thinks how it looks, looks how it….he took a notebook out of his book bag and started flipping through the pages of words, characters, and figures: last of the words, the bus stop, six eight zero three one, sixty four south, yellow dotted line road. seven seventy-six. ticket in the box.

    wha's like us. he put the book down and then under his arm and slung his bag on his back and walked on the bus. ticket in money box. to the metro. now. sitting beside everyone else going to and from: same time, different trip. a bus unit. driver makes twenty-four sixty an hour. about twenty people on the bus on different tickets, plans, reductions. nobody hangin on the side or sittin on the roof. relatively clean, stepped on metro daily newspapers. a coke can rolling around with every stop and turn and go and fast and slow laps around and in the metro. now.

a botched shaman, the black hippie, dealer's eye and edgar the honest aristotle

us like wha? mac had been awake and out of the house since eight thirty this morning. what he most definitely wasn't thinking about was waking consciousness, in the day. so he spent it on coffee, chocolate, bummed cigarettes, butts off the floor. he had an empty wooden crate that used to be filled with lettuce in his hand. he liked to smoke like shiva. a cigarette in his other hand. mac kept walking past the instacheque, the closed chinese noodle shop, a regular neighbourhood crackhead. brother just loves crack. no man. a life devoted to the fail.

busy afternoon downtown. he stopped on the block across from the university and sat down on the box, finishing his cigarette and eyeballing the passerbyers. listening to the conversations. french, english, arabic, spanish, cree, punjab. passing left. right. high heels. shopping bags, book bags, hand bags, in and out of everywhere. he flicked the cherry off the cigarette and put it behind his ear. took out a bandana from his back pocket and set it on the ground in front of him. raises to his feet, cracks his back and stands up on the crate.

the latest and fadest of em all! why tribulate? why oh why has thou shit and money mix like a copulation of de devil and de succubus, meridiana, you bordello bitch, you broke my heart, how can i ever repay you? beatin berta! berta! on our souls, the sins. berta! ellie may!

the block is now mac's, no red cross, s.p.c.a, unicef, falun gong, harikrishnas, or green peace.

decontextualized days possibly cause negative reactions to negative liberty. i'm no statue and torch, but not far from it, hybrid figurines in us all. the only question is—the only question is the only question. can i get a witness! good god! huh! dem small case letters are to capital letters like recreation is to domestication. domestics! our plebeian plight is in our voices! not in the titles ascribed to ownership! absolve this temple, this womb, no manifestation can caress us so. whether liberty bells on the mountain or liberty bells on your pie, your vaccinations and candy.

benefactors stand like drone centaurs with placenta flesh and fading coal for organs. a high commodity on the black market is transposed, transposition is the callin through como gospels and all down past and up the mississippi. m.i.s.s.i.s.s.i.p.p.i, transposed an acronym, a migrant worker, roma, everythin is an access. not always big enough to fit through pores, not always accustomed to the program or format presumed to be. presumptuous as lemmings, particular peculiarities and their peculiar particles, rampant and free to run off a cliff. no warnin signs for three hundred and fifty-six degrees around, maybe three hundred and fifty-seven. until three hundred and sixty! do the math! three or four to rest, only need one avenue. three or four? snap! a buffet! some people would slow down to listen to mac. on the other hand, the left hand, what law, if one existed, would allow us to gorge our bellies like idols of the beasts who were persecuted and sentenced to the abyss. jealous blasphemy!

he trembled and silenced himself. observing the pedestrians walking by. he put his hand beaked out over his eyes and squinted, trying to see as far as the eye could see.

he was looking about then saw a familiar face three blocks down. a bobbing body in the sidewalk's currents didn't yet see mac. mac stepped off the wooden crate and bummed a cigarette off someone, sat down attentively and let the smoke out through his nostrils. he speculated how real the fluid gestures of everything he saw and sensed were. drafts of(f) people, sounds vibrating the concrete below his feet. pupils not so dilated—masses splintered in the cone rays of his retina. for every fractal cone another memory, another day, another nother.

the bobbing body named bobby noticed mac. mista mac, wuddup? where you been? you know yo. they put me in for three weeks man! i've been out for a week now. fuckin vampires. shiiiit man. i left after i got thirteen people to walk out of there with me. ha! what? those people need to be let out. you know? one of em hadn't been outside in nine years. it's crazy man. ya mahn, sounds like madness. what are you sayin, then? not much, just been soapboxin for a minute. word, i'm gonna go get some 'za yo. yeah? i was thinkin the same thing a while ago. let's do this then. aright.

    they walked off the busy downtown street onto a calmer, shadier maisonneuve street. bobby lit a joint. they walked by a neighbourhood chinaman, so they figured, looked to be about sixty years-old. he always wore loose black clothing, his frame short and thin, carrying around a garbage bag or two filled with empty cans, stopping at every garbage can and garbage pile. they suppose the can man and his equally statured wife would work alternate days of the week since you wouldn't see them out on the same day.

    bunch of fucking sophists man. you know? what's that? i get in there and they just feed you sophistry. lotus flowers and lies. what are some of them like? oho man, zombies, shamans, a priest, a ghost stuck in a body. bobby laughs. check it out. what? bobby nodded his head towards a girl walking on the other side of the street. tall, long legs, middle eastern looking, dark curly hair. cot damn. uh huh. i think she just lives down the block, i see her almost everyday. bobby handed the joint to mac. sensitively sensible, just a little, sure. he took a few quick draws, trying a bit like it was his first time. he wouldn't know the outcome.

    are there any broads? inside? ye. a few nurses. i had an affair with one of the doctors once. an egyptian woman in her thirties. then one time her husband found us at a coffee shop and that was the last i saw of her. haha. what? bullshit mahn. ha. a million ideas came to mac's mind all at once, racing thoughts, he couldn't be bothered by the source of it all, he was happy with himself. decoding the daily manifestations and their cybernetic plots was time-consuming enough.

    bobby put the joint out under his shoe and exhaled a last haul. slipped it into a pack of smokes and pocketed. they

walked into the al taib. one cheese please. for you? one cheese. a drink? no thanks. a dollar seventy-five. thanks. a dollar seventy-five. the radio was playing arabic music when click click cl:i:lilililiiincoming transmission beeped over the song and bobby's cell rang.
    ostie, this girl's killin me mahn. i tried to get her to come out last night and she gets back to me today. every time. oh ya? she's fit man, that's why i keep askin her out. check it: i met her at the blue motel bout a month ago now. i never really go there but it was buddy's birthday. we roll in there at like eleven or something. we were waitin for delivery to come by with yayo. he gets there and i go to the bathroom for a key. the line up was too long to wait and i turn and start chattin with this girl. she says just do the key there. alright. then i offer her one. anyhow, i share the whole thing with her. she was lovin it. what thing? the yayo. at one point we're outside for a smoke. it was too windy so we end up in the back alley finishin the last keys. i tried to kiss her and all and she says, she's seein someone. she was a good girl though, respectable. she says we'll do a night together again. so yeah, i just ring her once and a while. i'd feel like a chump if she didn't message me back. now all i get are these messages. don't get the girl. i'll keep bein shameless, she likes it, the attention or something. i wouldn't be surprised if i never saw her again, i'll look up her name on my cell and…it's like an avatar. i get messages from a girl, i can barely remember what she looks like.
    makes sense, says mac. how? mac's mind would often weave in and out of a rhetoric of avatars. cycle-vincible and interchanging, double-overed hermeneutic. he could pick up earth in his palms and make it electric. static electric, electric static, one day you'll be able to plug anything into the floor we stand on. tesla terrestrial. decomposing rhetoric blocks and building root systems. mac claimed prana was being manipulated from the top of tibet to the sewers of rio's favelas. he blamed all the murderers who were like clergymen for some massive ritual taking place. that's also why he wouldn't work and his (en)doctrine made him a bachelor of this. touch the avatar and follow the chain linked helix of life,

ancestors, descendants, descending, ascending, link after link. this was his anti-gravity chamber of consciousness.

    love, mac started saying, that's what you're lookin for yo. ha, more like just a lay mahn. good one, layman, lover's layman, a layman of love. is that what we are? ye well at any rate, i gotta get some soon. your girl doesn't have any friends? let's get a party goin on. i dunno, not really, most of her friends are dudes. i got a few more digits to call up anyway. they sat at the terrace eating the pizza and then smoked a cigarette together, mac not having any as usual. the city was hot and muggy, the island city surrounded by the st. lawrence river.

    i was thinkin bout seein what edgar was up to. i was thinkin about him earlier, i thought i saw him at the croissanterie on the computer. oh yeah? yeah, just earlier, two hours ago. word word. mac tended to be selective about who and when he could be around certain people. i'm probly goin to go meet isabelle, he said. word, what are you up to later? i'm thinkin bout goin to the open mic. you should come man, i got some new poems i wrote last night. they just kept comin like prophecies, i couldn't sleep. lol, prophecies eh? ya man! you should come. ye, i'll try to make it by yo. ok man, well i'll see you later.

    mac got up and gave a cool limp handshake. word g, bobby exhaled the last of the cigarette and got up. they parted ways and mac disappeared into the sidewalk traffic.

    bobby casually walked onto the street and around the oncoming cars to get to the shady back roads on the way to edgar's. a hop skip onto the sidewalk and he recognized a dealer. bobby owed him a hundred and eighty bucks. he was often standing in front of the same fast food joint with a few of the same guys he was with now. muthafuckas. bobby hurried to get out of sight.

    and then the muthafucka beside him was like olive oil from popeye, arms up in the air and shit, stop! don't fight! don't fight! haha. he got away quick g. yeah but…oh shit, looks like he ain't the only one tryin to get away quick. that black ass punk hippie over there. yeah man, i gotta make a run in a minute, i don't have the time yo, this muthafucka's goin to have to wait, he told me he'd pay yesterday. full? muthafucka don't be askin me full!? who the fuck are you? don't worry about mine! alright? then dealer's phone beeped. word yo, that's me, i gotta run. aright g, word, ya mahn, ez, a+, check.

four blocks later and bobby walked under the stained glass door and through apartment doors. from the corner of his eye he caught sight of who he thought was one of the guys that was with dealer. hard to tell, but he was coming his way. bobby rang edgar's buzzer. the seconds passed. he looked out the door, he didn't see anyone. the buzzer rang up to the second floor. knock knock. yello? yeah! come in! in edgar's contorted and high-pitched voice: yo! wussup man?! one of the whitest boys alive.

man, how many hours do you spend playin that game? i try to limit myself to three hours a day. but who says i'm playing 'that' game? i could be reading the news, doing research, or watching porn…

cuz you look high as fuck and the screen is reflectin off your face. he walked past edgar, who didn't have the time to raise his head, and opened the blinds and window. what's happenin today man? not too sure yet. probly go watch the game at the sports station later. word. wanna hit betty? ye boi! out came the bong. five minutes later: bobby's sitting on the black leather sofa edgar's old man bought for him, it was basically the only piece of furniture in the double living room space.

ya mahn, you should get out of the house today and get some air, or beer, or both. how bout we go on the rooftop and chill out. i got twenty bucks, how bout we cut on a three and a half. i'll check my account too, i think i got more cash, then i'll go get beer. edgar chuckles. take it easy man, you really wanna get drunk do ya there buddy? naw man, as much as i wouldn't mind, but it's hot as a muthafucka out there, what else is better? i still need to have a shower and shit, just let me finish this game, i'll go with you. i need food anyway. word.

bobby stepped over to the other side of the living room and looked through the stacks of books on the floor. polanyi, land, gendlin, the twenty-first-century poetry for the twenty-second-century reader anthology, kellough, cohen. did you read all these? most of them. walter benjamin, a drug encyclopedia. junky bastard, i'm surprised you took the time to organize these in some kind of order. even got burroughs with the drug encyclopedia.

    i actually didn't organize them. phil came up from toronto with his girlfriend and her friend last weekend. i had an essay to finish, but i left my laptop at tommy's who had to work sunday night, so i had to go get it early. to make a long story short, i stepped out and they cleaned the place before they left, unless it was the landlady again. did you bang the friend or the landlady? again? ha! no, but she left a note on my bed. the landlady? no, morgan, the girl who came with phil's girl. but you did sleep with the landlady, too? i didn't sleep with the fucking landlady, man. lol. edgar moved to get up and froze in half motion. i got…and he leaned his face towards the screen. don't fall into the computer now, some muthafuckin jumangi rhizome. they both seemed to be overstanding, resolving pixels like the screen, emulsifying from the haze. laughs. edgar played kendrick lamar's adhd. i thought he was german or something at first. straight outta compton. uh huh. word. can i get on that for a minute? ya man. edgar went to the bathroom and bobby got on the computer.

this afternoon

calvin walked out of the metro with a coffee in one hand and a cig in the other. then he recognized mac with his back turned to him. but then suddenly mac turned around in a presumptive state. hey man, how's it goin? where you comin from? pounds. wuddup mac? just got downtown. are you workin today? naw man, got the day off and getting paid yo! quick slap handshake. niiiice. you goin out tonight then? i dunno. you should come to the open mic.

ye, maybe, no plans yet, which one you goin to? plus last time was too much black rhyming with black and so a glass ceiling onto another glass ceiling are more rooms so it boxes what it tries to achieve in this day and age like obama satisfies and there isn't the karma of a morrocan jew lost after losing the lost tribe of dan saying i don't get it. pride runs over and underground railways—used, obsolete, not forgotten.

i gotta keep movin man, gotta get to work before the boss leaves for the afternoon. ya man, i'm tryin to get a few people to come tonight, then we could have a party at mine or something. i just saw bobby. oh ye? word, well i'll call you later if i don't see you. ok man, peace. ya mahn. calvin was approached by someone else. excuse me, french or english, asked the stranger. no. calvin kept walking and mac turned and bobby! do you have a smoke for us? no. last one g, i gotta bounce, peace.

calvin walked around the block and lit his smoke. a girl from school days. two more girls. a chicano con he gave a beer to one night after chico said he just got out of jail and was high on mdma to celebrate his release. walking by a café where a guy on day leave from the hospital casually talks about his paranormal abilities, his breath could purify air he said while cigarette smoke rolled out of his mouth. so, he continued, the smoke i exhale isn't even bad for you. then another, and a car with a face, building faces, faces, faces, enter. the twenty-four hour asian-run computer/internet place.

shit. how much do i have left? seven seventy-six. hi, half an hour please. he paid two bucks and got appointed computer thirty-one. checking emails. junk. junk. notifications. nothing. man, when did i send it? eight weeks ago. i gotta write them again. ah synchronicity. an email just arrived from BARC poetry. it read,

dear calvin,

thanks for sending us this interview. although it is interesting, we're not sure if it's for us. who do you refer to as your 'target audience' for this interview? our publication is geared towards the everyday reader, your interview seems to be made for an academic audience.

thank you for considering us,
sincerely,
the BARC editorial staff.

    unbelievable. how much clearer does it have to be. where am i supposed to start if not by addressing the white reader. there's an ethnic ethic. he says it in the interview. he is speaking to everyone, not just white people, everyone. metaracial. logical forms are numberless—wittgenstein. but some of these people don't think it's important. that it doesn't speak to them. that it's not up to them. someone else will call the police while i hear the lady getting stabbed a hundred times in the alleyway. passive. pass. pass. passive. violence. it's driving me fucking mental! cal realized he was talking out loud and getting louder. he looked around him. nothing unfamiliar in the computer cafe. all the gamers were busy yelling at the screens anyway. i'll…what? um…mu? tahw…ll'i, um…pullin on them puppet strings. he logged out of his email. and your fingers are becoming cranes, he hummed, pullin on those puppet strings, yeah, yeah, yeah. why is that song in my head all of the sudden?

    transmitted dialect unplugged in the electric acoustics shivering through the room's anatomy, computer to person to static to transmission and what else? i and i and i for an i need to look up something else. when's that thing? right. click. snap. diffusion brought to you: next friday. k. 7:30 pm. word. still got twenty minutes left. would like a buck back. excuse me, yeah i only needed the computer for ten minutes, can i get a dollar back? no: policy: the clerk tapped his finger on the laminated paper taped to the counter: come on man, i come here all the time: the clerk kept staring at his screen: don't be a dick: fuckin eh, this is ridiculous: that would be ridiculous.

    calvin got up from his chair. thanks he said to the clerk, no response from the clerk as he stared at his screen and slurped his microwave noodles.

ço

bobby and edgar walk out of edgar's building. i just saw that piece of shit dwayne standin by mcdonalds before…see what i mean, is that or is that not one of his boys just standin at the end of the block? who? where? right there yo. i dunno man. i thought i saw him following me here before. let these cunts try something. they ain't got the science to catch me. he's walkin away now. what? you owe dwayne? ye, he smiled, one eighty. i just keep putting it off. now, check, he's gone. i dunno. i can see why you want a drink. i've recently discovered that there's a differentiation between what is called traditional alcoholism and the term problem drinker, and since i have no physical dependency, i fall into the category of the latter. is that so? indubitably. are you still looking for work? ya mahn, it's a bitch tryin to get a job right now. and there ain't no way i'm workin for some mcdonalds all summer.

 i was thinkin about losin my mind to get disability. i can will my way. that's not funny man. what? it's easy. you say you feel like you're going crazy and the psychologist will say, i'll refer you to a psychiatrist. it's as easy as that to get started. that's what happened to mac. do you think he's been programmed? programmed, eh? i would say he poses a sort of threat to….to the they. but he doesn't do anything really.

 they walk into the dep to buy refreshments. you hear the words that come out of his mouth sometimes? if you stop and listen to him, you'll hear it man. yeah, he poses a threat to time management, to the management of time and space, to the way we read time and to the way time and space is read to us. his words, they fizzle out the narrative of time and space. i thought about it the other day, it's like injecting words into time, it'll crumble—babylon. edgar chuckles while trying to figure out what he's going to drink. ah, babylon, again. bobby sings, it's that reggae music. fuck it, a forty it is. bobby grabs a forty ounce bottle of malt liquor. forties? you high class muthafucka, what's that? moretti, its italian, good beer, fresh, doesn't taste like piss. this shit'll put hair on your chest, boi. i don't know what i want to eat. we'll go to the grocery store after. sure mang.

 they approach the counter. hi. is that everything? ye.

separate though. bobby swipes his card into the interact console. fuckin eh, insufficient funds. cot damn. here, i've got cash, and he hands the cashier a ten. and three seventy-five is your change. then edgar pays. thirteen dollars. shamone, thirteen bucks, i gotta taste some of that. you can have one man. word. they walked back out into the sun.
    i miss hangin out at main's, said bobby, as they walked past their friend's old apartment. ye, where is he anyway? in paris, i think, i dunno if he went anywhere else for the summer, i haven't spoken to him in a few months. edgar pulled out a pouch of rolling tobacco and spun a cig. where are we going? fuck, i wanna see what the deal is with my account. you can check it on the computer when we get back. ye, i guess. so, um…where do you wanna get weed? i got a guy, delivery, we can call them. do they take long? usually like half an hour, max, i can make an order, you just gotta text them. oh ye? word, so let's turn around and go to the grocery store. k.
    they passed main's old apartment again. it was alright stayin at main's durin the winter. his cousin used to come over all the time, she was fine as hell. dalia. ohhh ya, i remember her from a party there. ya, you were there eh? fuck, that was my chance to get her, she came to bed with me but i was so smashed i couldn't even get it up. haha. i haven't touched the gin since. man, then i left like a week later. i never saw her again. main moved out after that too. ye. but it's alright sleepin on the mountain, i found myself a good spot. you leave your stuff there? ye. it's not like i own anything anyway, i just put my bag up in a tree. camouflaged and shit. that's alright then eh? uh huh. yep. no doot aboot it. bobby fell into a revery, back to dalia.
    he opened his forty and took a sip. so fresh. you mind if i get a drag? sure. they walked for two blocks, just short of being aimless, rambling and watching. the grid of blocks, the girls on bikes, the alleyways, car stereo systems rattling bass from trunk subwoofers, a city bus drove by. what are you gonna get. i dunno, i've been eating quinoa pretty often. hippy bastard. bobby smiled. it's good stuff though, malory got me on it because she

was allergic to gluten. gluten allergies man, all of the sudden everyone's allergic to gluten. but you get full and don't feel like shit after.

    they walked up to the PA grocery store. i'm just goin to chill here yo, i got everythin i need for now. k. edgar went into the shop while bobby sat in the shade on the building's stoop next door. he saw a cop cruiser rolling down the block. the two in the cruiser looked at bobby with his closed bottle in a paper bag. fuckin police. fuck the police, fuck em, fuck em, fuck the police…woop woop, it's the sounds of the beast…hello there, probly students, live up the block. hi. one smiled and they kept on walking past bobby. love to watch em come, but i like to watch em go as well.

    talkin bout a black seed, fear of the unknown / what you can't see, yo / i drip and spit braille blotter prints, i'm not a prince, but i got some of that highness / that dolce and gabbana ssshhh/shut the fuck up / bukka bukka, belly in jamaica, i'd like to visit but i got no paper / smoke and mirrors, bats and beers / can we call it my present state or the present years? / yo, i just gotta say, i'll go see what's around the way, hey, hey.

    he looked up and down the block, keeping a look out. urbania, exurbia, disturbia. out comes edgar from the store. if you're goin to be hypocritical you might as well be a hippy. what? bobby stood up and they strolled off the scene. i've heard that one before. did you get your thing? naw i just lifted this. dylan's probly in the library if you wanna go pick up. ah, well i already ordered. back to your's then. let's do this then. then then. when?

they hadn't been back at edgar's for five minutes when edgar got a call. hello? ok. 302. ya. that was quick as fuck. hook me up with that number man. the buzzer rang. how do you wanna sort this out? you got any change? i paid fifteen last time so… ok ok, i'll pay the fifteen. i gotta get my shit sorted at the bank. here. knock knock. k. edgar opened the door. hey man. the bike helmet wearing, septum pierced delivery guy walked in and began to take his knapsack off his back. wuddup man? bobby was sitting down on the couch and looked up from the laptop. yooo, wuddup g? bobby? what are you doin here? bobby laughed. workin hard for a better future eh? what kinda goods ya got for us today mayng? the delivery guy, ed, walked in. edgar closed the door behind him. ed put his bag on the floor, unzipped it and took out a tupperware. we got some cheese, purple kush, some m, afghan and shake. shake eh? how much? a three and a half for thirty, twenty-five for the m, fifteen for the shake. i got this red gum hash too. sounds beautiful. yo edgar. ye, i forgot it was thirty, here. he hands bobby the extra five and a ten. k. which one you think? take me to the land of kush.

   ya mahn. one kush then please and thank you kind sir. how do you guys know each other? um…i don't know, i guess from chillin on the canal, by herring's eh? ya, i guess so. word, well here you go man, thirty bucks. why don't you sit down and smoke a spliff with us g? uhhh, ye i got a few minutes. sure. word. make some space. ya mahn. you got a grinder? it's all over there, beside betty.

   the three of them sat in the hollow room on the black leather sofa and spun the new new. they talked a bit of bullshit until the kush was ignited, smoked, graded, complimented, coughed, compounded, cremated. the order of rotation was edgar, ed, then bobby. bobby passed the joint back to ed who in theory and practice should pass it in the proper order of rotation, no matter clockwise or counter, although clockwise, to the left is the proper. ed spoke: you know, smoking a joint in rotation is a good metaphor. if we sit in a line and pass it back and forth, i'll get more because i'm in the middle, if we distribute the joint equally in a rotation then everyone gets a fair share. puff puff pass is my motto.

    i got a motto, the shit ain't a microphone. pass it on. i would and will pass it on, i will not capitalize on such a fine example of communal economy. uh huh. ok, thanks for that. who's keepin count anyhow? i sure as hell ain't capitalizin on much else. i just provided the service of bringing it here. alright man, can we just smoke this joint then. just understand to oversee this, i don't need to hear this day in and day out. for the same reason that i don't do a lot of things with the assumption that it'll aaallll be better after. ye...bobby kept his cool, still, conveying. now all i'm tryin to say is that. in the meantime bobby had a few puffs and let the joint burn to roach. capital eyes yo. he leaned over and ashed the roach into an empty beer can. who's got their eyes on the capital? thanks for that, i gotta get goin guys. maybe see you guys down by the canal later. ya mahn, easy. ciao man. thanks. later. and out went ed as edgar closed the door behind him.

    edgar walked over and grabbed two beers from beside the door. cheers. they heard the lobby door close. without wasting a step in his direction he went over to the window and saw ed roll off on his bike. i'm just tryin to chill out, you know. sometimes these cunts start talkin like they want you to go out on the street and start protestin right away, all those people, all those numbers, all self-righteous, end up smashin the windows of the bank their student loan gets transferred to. here's an idea, take your student loans and make your own school. make a business. that would be a joke. how many students are there gettin loans? one year, everyone just put your money together and do you. hire your own teachers. teach yourselves. the entire humanities department can get away with that. they don't need science labs. the streets is the science lab. the internet is the platform. youtube lectures. everything. peer-reviewed work. that's what they do and this is what i do. what's that? fuck babylon. in fact, fuck the bank, i don't need it anymore. half of it's bullshit. everyone's busy spending their money tryin to figure out how to stop the problem but nobody has the balls to just stop. stop payin your debt. stop playin by babylon's rules. nobody ever beat a system by playin by the system's rules. gandhi? india's still colonized by the banks. MLK? babylon didn't care when he was talkin about race, he got killed when he started talkin about class and fuckin with the idea of babylon's pockets! brothers still gettin shot by the police, systematically lynched. and on that tip, buy guns, cuz you know who's goin to come after you with guns. nothin is better, we're all just bendin over a little bit more and gettin worked in so often that we're used to it and probly some even enjoy gettin fucked cause they're lookin around and being like, at least i'm not that poor motherfucker, he's got it real bad, but me, i'm not so bad, so it's okay. it's not okay! we got the numbers to support each other. passing the blame on to someone else, lettin this pass, lettin that pass. god damn gandolf said it, you shall not pass! and who's the hero of that story, the littlest feeble hobbit. and he stopped. in fact, he went and straight up threw that power and privilege he had into the fire, right back in the face of the enemy. shit man. alright alright, edgar passed bobby a beer. so we go jam on the roof then? i'm down. word.

  edgar went to his bedroom and came out with two acoustic guitars. they went out the kitchen door and up the fire escape to the roof. would the will to do something or nothing change anything? could it be better? just be, but be.

☙

the dealer sat on a bench in the west end neighbourhood of n.d.g. behind him was the park he used to play in as a child. around the corner was his first apartment he rented at seventeen years old. he was supposed to meet at this bench but the guy was late. muthafucka makin me wait like this. he looked at the time on his cell. the client/partner was a regular, a twenty something year old playboy from the west island who still lived in his parent's house. he drove a brand new gold volvo that his parents gave him after graduating from university. maybe he was too much of a mama's boy and didn't want to leave the house and couldn't take a hint that they bought him the car to drive off and leave the house. or it could be that he was simply conniving enough to fool his folks into thinking he had a night job while he was actually driving around hustling.

  there were quite a few people walking around the dealers old neighbourhood. he didn't feel like running into any old friends, or enemies, and he began to reconsider agreeing to choose this place for a meeting spot. it was close to the playboy's chop shop he knew that. that's where some of his runners did shift work day and night.

the dealer sat smoking a cigarette, keeping an eye out for anyone and anything. he turned his head and the car pulled up in front of him. the tinted window rolled down. wuddup homie, said the playboy in a polo shirt, gelled hair, tennis shoes, rayban glasses. dealer got up, approached the car, wuddup man? and got in. they started driving down the block and dealer pulled an ounce out of his boxers and placed it on the surface between the two front seats. this is the primo g. just a sniff and you're bleezed for an hour. i know you always got the product man, that's why you're my man, man, and playboy laughed with self-satisfaction.

dealer figured the guy was always high or had spent the greater part of his school funds that his parents saved for him on getting high. he started up his business while getting high on his own supply. if he wants to hustle let him be to be the act he see.

playboy's phone rang, he looked at the caller i.d., who's this? just a second yo. hello? ya mahn, lemme call you back in a couple of minutes. k. ciao. they turned right and circled the park. and this is for you. he handed dealer an envelope. dealer took a quick look inside and fingered the bills. seventeen fifty? no doubt g. word. you need a lift somewhere. naw man. i'm aright. even though dealer was known by most as the hookup he always managed to keep a low profile. no car, no jewellery, a modest apartment he shared with his girl. he got a certain respect from others for this modesty, but as the game turns: to contain modesty and diligence in the midst of stress, the body reacts, and the environment around it, more bodies, tissue, skin of skin, rock, metal, these were all combustible, they could all be corrosive or corrode and dance to crumbs of dust. it just depends on, it just depends off. a simple game, like nature. its fruit, its seasons, its chaos and uncertainty, the dealer orbited around his preferred elements while the other elements provided their nourishment and poison. there was nothing convoluted, there was only raw, what wasn't spoken is never said, only acts playing, resonating deeper than anything he knew of god, and that was what sounded from within him.

    i'll just get out over here. he pointed. word. the car stopped. aright man, hey i'm throwin a party this weekend. oh ye, word. send me a text with the info. is it downtown? naw bro, up north at my parent's cottage. we'll see. holler. word. word one. dealer steps out the car.

❧

di be do ba day. calvin swiped his card to enter the employee entrance of the big ol hotel he worked in. that ink was just fresh off the big bosses bald point, gold tipped, initialed pen. sure right it was.

    so anyhow, cal walks in and sees charlie, hey hey cal kale, kale cal. what's up? fuckin the dog charlie? i'm goin out for a smoke, you want? if you wait we can smoke a joint. aw man, i've been takin a shit for the past 15 minutes…okay okay, i'll be back in a minute if all goes well. aright cal kale, check ya later! cal kept on going down the stairs. to the right was the cafeteria. good food, sometimes you could have a buffet if you already swiped your card once for five twenty five a day deducted from your pay, along with the union dues, pension plan, gst, hst, pst, qst, fxt, xst. chuckles.

    so down he goes past some chambermaids, a fine young costa rican girl he'd been eyein for some time. chuckles. ya, then he turns into the laundry department to go see the boss. now ya had all sorts of huge machines here. the place musta been as big as a football field. in the back you had five industrial washin machines, four four hundred pound capacity machines and one two hundred and twenty five pounder -- of dirty laundry. now i don't mean pants and panties, i mean all the pillowcases, the bed sheets, dirty towels, face clothes and all the stuff. then you had the four hundred pounder dryer, but you only put towels and bed spreads in that. the rest would go through the presses, ironed and warm, nothing like a pillow case hot out the press, the clothing presses and the boss's office. oh yeah plus the little sewin room.

cal was one of them folks that rolled up his money in his sock, under the mattress, in an old pringles box, anythin. every second week he went to go collect his pay from the boss, mr. kelphasse. this day though, the boss maybe felt the need for some cosmetics or i don't know what cuz he was sittin in his chair with half his eyebrows all waxed off. he was already bald, now the man looked like a real dick.

cal sat down in the chair in front of kelphasse and smiled, holdin back from laughin. how are we today calvin? uh, fine, yourself? his eyebrows, bouncin up and down. is he waitin for me to say something about his face? good, thank you. and how may i help you? i'd like to get my pay. oh yes, your special cheque. it was just delivered from the director's office. i was told there is an additional letter inside the envelope for you to read. then he hands cal the envelope. is that so? kelphasse's face, man, those eyebrows were just dancing up and down like leeches bein electrocuted or something, he wanted to know what that letter said. he sat up on the very edge of his seat, hell, his ass wasn't even touchin the seat, he could of well missed it if he would actually sit back down on it. first cal looked at the cheque. then he started readin the letter. the boss gave him a minute to read it over and he knew damn well the union wouldn't let him ask what that paper said. cal just folded it back up and put in in the envelope with his pay.

calvin, may i ask you what happened last sunday? last sunday? yes, the system says you were an hour and sixteen minutes late. why is that? the man knew damn well why, he was just bein a prick now and for always. my phone died, i set the wrong time, the bus was late, the metro stopped, i had to buy somethin important. cuz i slept in. you slept in calvin? i slept in. i have no choice but to give you a suspension of one day. you have already received three verbal warnings, and i would say you're not off to a very good start in our hotel. thank god i'm unionized then eh? pardon me? the union is good.

cal got into the union after his first three weeks of preliminaries workin at the hotel. the boy made mistakes, or you can look at em like that, but they sure was measured mistakes. this was his fourth mistake in three and a half months. if you recognize your error and accept the consequence then you can agree by signing your name on this report, beside the x. the boss didn't bring in a union rep as a witness, cal knew boss wasn't playin by the rules, but he could care less, no use tryin or lyin to em about something so petty. he gave him his name in ink on the paper. is that it? i won't be here next friday because i have an appointment, so i'll be seeing you saturday morning at 8:45 am. ye, probly. he got up to leave the office, thanks.

    kelphasse just looked at cal like he was about to crack. our boy folded up his envelope, put it in his back pocket and closed the door behind him. call continued on out the laundry department. see you guys on saturday, he said to the crew. he went into the locker rooms for a piss. on his way down the aisles of lockers were a few guys takin naps on benches. then he heard someone, that guy nobody ever saw leave the shitter, and as usual it sounded like he was givin birth. it ain't good to force it. not natural.

    once he got back onto the street cal thought about the time. it was a day off, what was he rushin to do? naw, he thought, he'd best go cash that cheque now and get that money. he made his way to the money mart. they taxed seven percent to cash a cheque. that's the price you gotta pay, it ain't that bad, who else was goin to cash it? the bank? chuckles. no talkin sense into the boy about banks. he was hard headed alright. maybe a little introvert, but some just didn't understand his logic. the nice thing was that the liquor store was right across the street from the money mart. a mickey from a fresh new pay, save it for a rainy day like – money off a tree – your name's dead for the better, best born birthed to wake up with your eyes wide open, every picture you see, and build em, and you along with em too. the next time, the next one, the next thing to fix on or off – it's only goin to be the two you might think, but, there's always a but, there's always a but, but still. chuckles. it's a clue, a possibility in acquirin a grain of salt for you're lickin off of, or on to. chuckles. that proverb of a boat that floats in the lake playin if i had a million dollars he'd be rich over and over again...sittin on the beach, mindin your business. you sittin there, part of it all, you're in a big room called a world. those other rooms? let me tell you something...

    this boi would spend his last five dollars on a cold beer, there was nothin too blue about him, he was more like one of those blue worn out neon lights that flickers the name of a lost stop bootlegging bodega at the end of the night. the name ain't lightin up all the time but you sure can depend on what's inside. chuckles. where was he goin to get a beer? grumpys? it'd be no surprise to anyone who would see him there, so cal thought of findin a quieter place for that meanderin mind of his. andrew's pub? alice's? naw, he went to the dep our other two boys had just gone to and he picked himself up a quart bottle. spendin money to get his money, spendin, spent again, now he was ready for the park. a small park tucked in a corner of downtown. and just like that money tree, the money fallin and scatterin, bein spent, his rambling footsteps counted him getting to where he was needin to go. cal knew he would pay with that money he had – he had to (s)pen(d) something. a mix like, wantin and havin to, not bein scared of not bein able, more so to see what would happen at the end of it all. he wouldn't die, he figured babylon wouldn't let him.

    by the time cal got to the park he felt that sense of being implicated, like while you're sittin on the beach and all you hear is that cot damn boat. he was is some:

urbania, exurbia, disturbia, the senses / in the end the shit and chaos is as enjoyable as colonization and industrialized relocation / lay the body down [as he would sip his beer in the shade, under a tree, starin past all the city in front of him, smoke rollin down and out the hills of his body] in the machine. favour the deconstruction of romanticism / loves becomes masochistic and vanglorious/ all in one day, and no one weeps / only look at the shit once and it's enough to tame the waking crush of luxury that affords a face, a masthead, callin itself humanity.

the boys back on the roof were getting on with the afternoon, the only thing measuring time was the emptiness to fullness of the beers they were drinkin and the number of tunes they'd played. then suddenly, sure as always, someone rang edgar. he put down his guitar. he kept his tone brisk and to the point: hello? ya, hey man, what's up? bobby kept playin the chords they'd started and sang: i'm broke again, i got drunk with my friends and now i'm broke again, i just got laid off and now i'm broke again, ill use my last pay to get gone again: yeah, we're just chillin man, on the roof…to be broke again, he would fly somewhere and be broke again…yeah man, probly later, you can pass by though: why should we stay here to be broke again. oh okay , cool duderoonie, talk to ya later, ciao man: i can't be fucked to find a better plan… what's the deal man? bobby said, still playin, did you find us some women to…to have fun with friend? chuckles. naw it was marcos, he's bored at work, they don't get any customers. where's he workin? i dunno, some restaurant uptown. uptown girls, i wanna get me some of them uptown girls. what were the words to that song you were playing? ya like that one eh? a little ting i be workin on mahn…i'm broke again…

stoopin it with a hobo fugue

i think i might go get another bottle. what time is it? about seven o clock. edgar'll probly be back in a while. ye. i dunno how i left that shit at his place. relax man, i got some. is that so? you been holdin out on me? you know i got you covered yo…whenever i can. word g. are you still leavin town? ya yo, tomorrow. really? shiiiit. how you goin to get there? he sticks out his thumb, hitchin. oh ye? definitely. i haven't hitchhiked in years now. fuck, how long do you think it'll take? hopefully get a lift right across, that's the dream ride anyway.

last time it took me a week. that's not too bad. i've heard people say it took em like three weeks though. the trains are good cuz you don't have to talk to anyone. sometimes i just can't be fucked havin conversation. and i've been downloadin music all week, enough not to have to listen to the same thing twice. made a mixtape of mash-ups too. n.w.a and woodie gutherie, some robert johnson on a track i made, sam cooke and tom waits, wu-tang and buena vista. even some shit no one heard of like baby huey, bringin the shit back man. you want one? fugue pulled out a cassette. ha! a cassette? what the fuck am i goin to do with this? you got a link. ya. just tryin to keep it old school you know. fugue wrote the link down on a paper and gave it to bobby. word.

how long you goin for? i dunno…gotta love the hobo life, stabbing people with my hobo knife. laughs. the simpsons. laughs.

you got any skins? ya mahn, i didn't even notice you bitin that up. cheers. you goin to work out there? not if i don't have to, probly just busk, usually gets me by. word word. word word?

bound to the bond like the five fingers and palm/ arm, leg, leg, arm and head/ my allah, (together they say) sorry i am infidel/ no justice, criminal, keepin liminal, coax the coasts of my body poor but righteous, i disown but invite any opposition that wants to fight this.

ya mahn. respect. you got a light? ya mahn.

you heard about the eclipse, i think it's in like a week or two. oh ye? naw, i didn't know. don't pay much attention to the stars and what not. it's a pretty impressive thing to see. a total solar eclipse, a syzygy yo. it'll be the sun, the earth and the moon. a what? syzygy, it'll be heavy. when three celestial bodies line up. the spring tide'll be massive in tofino, those surfer cunts'll be crawlin all over the place. hippie bastards. look who's talkin, the only person i know livin on the mountain. it's by choice. i ain't no hippie, why pay for rent when it's nice outside?

the ancient chinese yo, they'd beat on mirrors like drums to scare the dragon who ate the sun, so it'd spit it back up. durin the eclipse. here. i read they figured out that gravity can affect time,

time actually slows down near a massive body. it's all relative. ye, it's quantum shit. like this tesseract mang. it's the way the mind works. and that's why it's real, because i can imagine it. the crystal of the mind. the hobo took out a scrappy notebook and opened it up to show bobby:

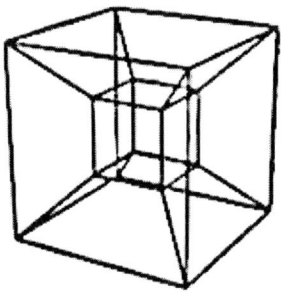

    it's the fourth dimension, a hyper cube. What box have you been living in? what virtual reality have you created? Or has been created, programmed for you? we're meant to explore em, not be trapped slavin for one program. That's where we're supposed to go, for now, I think. We each become programmers of reality, virtual realities of a microcosm in our macrocosmic sphere of microcosms. We're goin to go into the great unknown of the known. Can't fear loss of self, you only gain knowledge of self. Of our minds. The life of our minds.

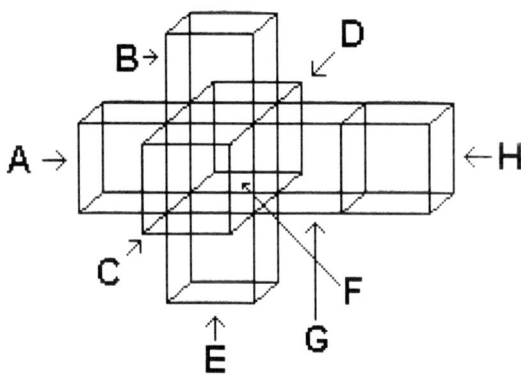

where you goin with all this? It's all after canaan mang. only time can tell, unless my body's big enough to slow it down, or the body I am an organ of. but then i'll probly be dead before time tells me anything. right, cuz the time time takes…does it go faster? slower? if it goes too fast we die fast, if it goes too slow? i'm pretty happy with time. for the moment? for always… what the fuck eh. no, but i get it, kinda. space-time muthafucka. really tho, it proves that time isn't constant, that it's influenced by bodies, by selves, by i & i. you and i. yes, i. supposedly they gotta be massive, but still. it varies accordin to the distribution of bodies. The problem and solution is that we're i-cubed yo, like this (and he pointed in his notebook): i^3. the problem and the solution?

you heard about the chemtrails? ya ya, rolls his eyes, no need to start with that conspiracy shit. ha! and what are you talkin about? it ain't the same, ain't no chemical alchemy or science controlling gravity any time soon. These ideas, theories of these bodies, are they like our bodies? does the body know, or is it getting pulled by the gravitational force of time, and all the bodies of history? huh? it all just comes to you, seek and you will find.

where'd you get this shit man, i am blitzed. laughs. it's alright eh? in the east end, it's the hell's shit. hot damn. can you hook it up? i dunno, probly. but i'm leavin tomorrow, i'd have to bring you to introduce you to the guy. double damn. swing me from the pendulum, that elliptical track, pull me off the earth so time can turn back. ain't no goin back, ah, but yeah, i'm overstandin the understandin. jah mahn. it's that babylon man, extortin our evolution. they hold us back, down, it does, changing the gravity of the situation, changing the gravity of our lives, makin us orbit around all their priorities and programs. Right mang? Like makin us forget who we are. pullin us in, windin time to tight to get out. babylon, ya mahn, how high they tryin to build? it'll topple. everyone knows it, so they think recycling their garbage is goin to help the problem?! naw man, that's the right idea, preservation vs. expansion. neitzsche. oh ye? ya mahn. we're movin beyond good and evil. cuz that's what's up these days, over simplifyin everythin, he noticed that like more than a hundred years ago. god is dead, "man" is dead, just like hip hop. but that don't mean it ain't still alive. true say. but it failed to bring what it said it would. we gotta articulate the new biologism. the next level shit. cuz the truth is beyond the good and the bad, taste, evil, that's how it makes sense. rastafari knows what's up.

    some folks, you start talkin babylon and then they say ya ya babylon, you like to smoke weed eh? babylon eh, it's easy to say, easy to blame. but then, who am i tryin to blame? america? the colonizers? the bible? nebuchadnezzar ii? ye, obviously you can blame the past, for fuck's sake man. ya mahn, the past, hip hop, it's still here, it might be dead, ye, europe raped and pillaged, they took everythin, "it" took everythin over here and called it their own…what, who, they didn't call their own they killed, i can't even waste my energy on getting pissed off about this kinda shit. how am i supposed to, how are we supposed to deal with the shit, i sure as hell ain't goin to get rich and not give a fuck. there ain't nothin wrong with havin money though. but too much money. look at the people who have too much, they turn. they get defensive, cuz people hate on em. it's normal. it's the cycle. they're scared. or they act fearless cuz of all the money they got. shit, look at us anyway. broke as fuck. is it by choice or by trade? the nature or nurture? bof, ya man, i dunno.

    i'll probly pick cherries in the okanagan for a few weeks. hopefully under the table. some of em make like two fifty a day, seven days a week. shamone!? they live off that for the whole year some of em, then they go back the next year, like some of those punks with the dogs and shit. some people go travel the world, some of em don't save a dime and spend all their money getting fucked up and havin fun before they get anywhere, or the junkies and crack heads go to vancouver for vacation. it's a funny little world over there, but everyone does their thing.

huh, crazy. i'll probly just stay here yo. ain't nothing like a montreal summer. well if you wanna get outta here it's always a good option. you wake up at five or six, work till eleven or noon, then you go lounge on the lake all afternoon. like i said, the fruit pickin season is like some clandestino paradise, people from all over the world there to just make some money, some wanna disappear. you got my contact eh? ye, the book of faces. word man, well lemme know if you change your mind, i'll sort you out. cheers man. as always. i gotta get movin g, a few more things to do, people to see before i leave. ok g, thanks for the spliff. ain't no thing brother. word. bonne voyage man. ya mahn, be well. check. check.

...pardon my behaviour, truly. you see, i have been harbouring sentiments of alienation for quite some time. i love you. that is why. as if life was fantastical, i've tried to redeem myself for you in vain. then you understand, i am a bastard. a fanatic who lost sight of the proverbial hills we supposedly wanted to elope to long ago. before christ and mohammedi's songs were consecrated. our relation was literal then figurative then literal again. i abolished the pacifists out of fear. this isn't a proclamation, for i know not what i do, i have only done. my reins have been held by the trife, the brave, the arrogant, the flamboyant. i cannot remember without malice. their titles and names, our saddles and fame, no, infamous – no, vigilante? i thought we would over come! oh but no, patting palms in the night, raping for braille to no avail but the ephemeral temperaments you've grown to know me by. you and i, we or someone else? something? to be the anonymous and quixotic wonder: the rabblement at her execution, the panged labourer vouching to cast the last stone moments before he collapses from inebriation, the sprawl of budding opiates, our tongues sworn into secrecy, holding back the tears of joy displayed – rehearsed polyglot illiterates buried under pyramids in sand and jungle, snow and stars. if i reach out i will not do so with the intention to singe flesh. i cannot ask for forgiveness because you will not grant me such serenity. and now we hack away more than ever. bangladesh to dakar trod on, mild aspirations of our intercontinental, metatextual

race. mild because of this, that, mild but forlorn. mild because we cannot situate the pressure. allow me to alleviate the sins i define with a boisterous commerce i know you'd wish to barter away on a black market – our souls, our bodies, our homes and our temples. let them shift, i will watch, omniscient and whole until my brother, my crutch, gives way and i and i and i faulter and grasp to clutch at oscillation://

the pub

it was goin on nine pm when cal and bobby walked into the bar. there were a few folks in there. kids with their guitars, comedians scribblin down jokes, a poet from outta town sittin solemnly near the end of the bar, sippin on a jameson, one of those pretty girls who would sit there all night and get hit on by different guys to let them buy her drinks, a couple of hipsters that seemed to be showin up more and more often in the what used to be a place where they were rarely found.

sook, cal addressed the bartender and shook his hand traditionally. cal. hey man, said bobby to sook. you got my money? asked sook. bobby had an outstanding bar tab that he'd been runnin since he got fired from his job last month. no, but i start workin next week. that was a lie. then what do you want from me? can you let me go till next week? sook was agitated, as usual, years of bein a bartender, late night shut-ins and whiskey, more whiskey, and beers, who knew how hungover he could have been, besides, he had to deal with people like bobby.

cal cut in, i'll get these ones sook. cheers man, said bobby. i'll just want two pints on it anyway sook. i've heard that from you for the past month, he looked to ignore bobby and asked cal, what'll it be? two jamies and two blondes, please. sook turned around and got the drinks ready. you want one sook? i'm okay, and he creaked his neck like he was hurtin from the night before. cheers there mista sook. cal and bobby raised the shots of jameson, looked each other in the eye, salut, cheers, and slugged em back.

    how's the list lookin for tonight? sook put the sign-up list for the open mic on the bar and the two of em glanced over the names. mac's already been here. ha. ye i saw him earlier. ye, so did i. you goin up? naw i don't think so, said cal. i got a few tunes i wanna sing, so bobby signed up at number ten. don't know if i want to afford sittin here till then. ah come on man. smoke then? ya mahn. they went out past the stage, the washrooms and the dartboard to the back patio.

    the only others sittin back there were tina and a friend of hers they'd never seen before. why hello there, said bobby. how yo doin tina? bobby and tina gave bisous. hey bobby, hey cal. hey tina. this is maggie. maggie, bobby and cal. hey there, nice to meet you. hi. cal smiled almost bashfully. oh la la, he thought. mind if we sit with you guys? no no, not at all. what are you ladies up to tonight? this. funny to bump into you here isn't it? tina rolled her eyes and smiled, yes bobby, quite the coincidence. coincidence indeed, the days been full of em. really? ya, and then we all find ourselves here, like it wasn't supposed to be.

    so maggie, how are you fortunate enough to know tina? from school, we just finished class a while ago. you guys in the same program? ya. that's cool. cal took out his rolling tobacco and spun one. can i? asked bobby. ya mahn. look at you, said maggie, mind if i get one of those too there cowboy? go right on ahead. thanks. she was gleeful about the novelty of a rolled cigarette. here, you can have this one. he handed her the smoke he just rolled and took his lighter out to light it for her. raised it up to her. lit it for her.

    how goes the summer? well we have summer school. must be hard to make it some days, on a day like today? ya well i'll graduate after this though. is that so? congratulations. what are you goin to do after? i dunno. seems to be the way things work. did you graduate yet? naw, took me a few years and a couple of grand later to realize it's not for me. i'm more of an autodidactic you know. i've heard that before. ya ya. how bout you come to b.c. with me when you're done and pick cherries. i heard you can make like two hundred and fifty bucks a day.

i'm probly going to take a trip to europe i was thinking. spain maybe. oh ye? asked cal, how much is it to get over there? i saw some tickets around five or six hundred. my parents said they'd buy me the ticket for graduating. lucky girl.

the game, the chase, the four of them knew it, the girls were on guard. do you go to school too, asked maggie. naw, i'm a workin man. oh yeah? what do you do? i work in a hotel, the king james. ooo fancy. ye it's alright. make good money. cal's a poet, bobby splurted. really? maggie was interested and looked at cal. ya, one of the best around. can you read me one of your poems? um. oh come on! i'm just tryin to think of one. here, let me see what i got. i've got new one's with me now, but most of em aren't finished.

and he went into his backpack fishing for his notebook. the three others waited attentively and then bobby spoke: i was tryin to get him to go up tonight. ye, but for the same reason i won't is cuz i don't have anything ready. i thought poets are supposed to know everythin off the top of their head? ya, well i don't really care what people think poets are supposed to do or what they should be able to do.

you hear that? that's why he's one of the best, he doesn't give a fuck. they all laughed as cal fished through his bag, taking out his belongings and putting them on the table. some food in a grocery bag and two books: collected rimbaud and a book about basquiat. oh i love basquiat, he's so sexy. yeah? well, there's a bit more to him that that. in my opinion he's one of the most important artists of the past one hundred years. look at this. and he left his bag and flipped through the pages. riding with death. and he was a cool muthafucka. played music and all. he fucked madonna too. who didn't? hahaha.

yo cal, did you see edgar today? nope. the guy disappeared. i waited for him to come back to his place. i think he should show up tonight. ye. you got any spliffs. i wish. you girls wouldn't happen to have any joints would you? nooo, let me know if you get some though. word. the open mic usually kicked off by ten. the four sat at the table and chatted while the patrons and vagrants of the bar started to scuttle around. they moved inside to get a table. another round of jamesons and a few pints later. the comedians performed first. weed jokes, self depricative jokes, dirty jokes, i can't believe he just said that of the politically incorrect kinda jokes. it may be the hardest of all forms of entertainment. if the crowd doesn't laugh, snicker, or at least smile, you're not that funny. and then they would have to deal with the hecklers, and there was nothing worse that getting out done by a heckler. hey, i don't do much stand up, that's why i sit down. ha!

there was one act before mac was supposed to go up. a newbie to the bar, he probably just heard there was an open mic, he'd soon find out how open the sceny bar could be. he was dressed of the hip hop persuasion. fitted baseball cap, a hoodie. hey, he asked sook through the microphone, how can i plug up my mp3 player? sook looked at him and didn't say a word, annoyed just by the fact he was bein called out through the amplifiers. he trodded out from behind the bar and jacked the mp3 player into the mixer and went back and stood behind the bar and wearily glared at the guy on the stage while he flicked through the mp3s to find the right track. everyone knew what was coming. some didn't mind. the boom bap and all that beat busted out of the amplifiers. the rapper started spittin his intro lyrics like: yo, what's up grumpys? my name's emcee adao and i'm here to say. boom! and the bass beat kicked in and he started rappin at a mile a minute.

before he could get through his first four bars sook walked back up from behind the bar and shut the sound off. the rapper and sook, hunched in his vest and button shirt like a city slickin cowboy, stood side by side. what the fuck man? what the fuck, replied sook. i don't like it. i'm not in the mood to listen to your shit either. sook turned around and went back behind the bar and served himself a whiskey. he left the dumbfounded rapper on the stage by himself as the mc of the open mic came up and reluctantly took the mic out of the rappers hand. sorry about that, the host said with his and over the mic. some of the patrons were too drunk to be paying attention to what just happened, a few others looked at each other like, did you just see that? the host hurried to continue the show a.s.a.p.

okay, next up on the list of fine performers this evening is mac. mac, come on down. mac, ladies and gentlemen, has anyone seen mac? bobby, cal and tina now sat by a table near the stage while maggie used the washroom. mac had never shown up. bobby stood up and said mac said i could take his place. okay. ladies and gents, please sit and prepare yourselves for the laid back debaucheries of none other than, bobby! a few applauds. bobby got up and sat down on the stool in front of the mic. and how bout a round of applauds for our handsome and gracious host. he turned and grabbed the house guitar. he tuned it while saying: i have a lovely ballad i hope you'll all enjoy and relate to. it's about the wife of god. you know the world would be a better place if god got laid. he got a few chuckles from the crowd. tina looked at him differently now, he was no longer the homeless, unemployed and most often enough inebriated bum that people saw him as. he glowed. it was probly this moment, this minor epiphany, that often allowed bobby to go back to tina's with her at the end of the night. and bobby started playing:

> if mary was black, then jesus was black
> but time's gone on and we can't go back
> black madonna, don't you wanna
> tell me somethin bout myself
> tell me somethin bout myself
>
> one man's fear is another man's prison
> it all can't be one man's wisdom
> maybe a lady lost in the story
> who's guilty? who stole the glory?

we all know it's a babylon system
if you don't then sit and listen
black madonna, don't you wanna
tell me somethin bout myself
tell me somethin bout myself
tell me somethin bout myself
tell me somethin bout myself

    when bobby finished and looked around the bar, there were about half as many people that he remembered seeing when he went up on stage. still, people were clapping. calvin, tina and maggie were hootin and a hollerin. thank you, thank you. bobby seemed quite pleased with himself and the response that he got. even sook seemed to respond positively by offering him a shot of jameson on the house once he got off stage. the host tried to coax him to get back on and sing another song. always leave em wantin more man, that's that name of the game ain't it?
    ladies and gentlemen give another round of applauds for bobby. suddenly i don't feel so bad spending the greater part of my life drinking away in this bar. hahaha. shit boi! said calvin to bobby when he sat back down at the table, where'd that come from? i wrote it. really? said tina, her eyes glowing, half drunk, admiring bobby. ain't nothin but a truth. cuz i'm a loser baby, so why don't ya kill me? huh. haha.
    the four of them were all jolly and drunk now. it was nearing half past eleven. shit man, i gotta catch the last metro. what time is it? fuck. where do you live? maggie asked cal. the end of the orange line, and a bus. ohhhh, man, that's so far. maggie and cal sat while bobby started necking tina. ya, tina said, i gotta work tomorrow. ahhh it's still early blurted bobby. well some of us have responsibilities bobby. he thought about that for a second. best to keep his mouth shut to better his odds at getting laid? speak his mind and piss her off? wait till they left the bar and say something to her when they were alone to make himself seem as though he was just down on his luck and that he was really a good guy? it's not like i don't want responsibility. i enjoy bein

a loser. i indulge in my inadequacies so that i don't have to face responsibility. am i a coward? immature? do i need a degree to impress anyone? fuckin eh.

    tina already turned around to talk to maggie. do you wanna go? nooo, let's stay for another. okay, do you want to come outside for a smoke then? sure. i'll join you guys, just gotta go to the bathroom. the two girls went out. as soon as they walked out the door: you hear that shit man, takin the piss outta me about responsibility and shit. relax man, i don't think she meant anythin by it. bof, i'm goin to try and get her back to hers tonight. she likes it.

    outside: sooo, you and calvin eh? giggles. what, well he is kinda cute. how long have you known him? for a few years, mostly from here. he likes you though. inside: how bout maggie huh? huh? he pried. she's quite the fine little thing. ya, she used to be with diego, i think, i used to see em together all the time anyway. fuck man, i gotta get outta my grandma's place. i gotta move downtown. do it like they do on the discovery channel man, laughs. Ye. but then i'm fucked and got no where to go. true true. outside: i don't know if bobby even has a place anymore, i heard he's been sleeping around on the mountain. bihihi, oooh, this is the bobby you were telling me about? ya, she said kind of reluctantly. you should take him in, giggles, like a stray puppy, they giggled together. mmm, but he sure is caliente in bed. oh?

    then tina and maggie were spotted by two guys at another table. tina looked over and saw them both looking at them. one of the two stood up and walked over to them. hey, do you guys have a light? thanks. inside: k, i just gotta take a piss, said cal. bobby went outside. outside: how you girls doing tonight? having fun? fine, ya. just hanging out. are any of you going up to sing tonight? no. no. you both look like the singing type, bet you sound as pretty as you look. bobby stepped out at the same moment. what's this? he walked up and put his arm around tina's shoulder. then he looked at the guy, hey man. thanks for the light, said the guy. he smiled at the two girls and went back to his table.

was that guy tryin to get as fresh as his breath? probably, tina replied non-chalantly. so how bout that round eh? inside: hey sook, can i get a jamie and a blonde please...cheers. outside: man, edgar never showed, or mac. i forgot my chronic at edgars. i need to call him. he rang him up and: yo man, what's good eh? where you at? cal comes out. shiiit boi, we were waitin for you. oh ye? cool. i'm with cal. you know tina? ya, and her friend maggie. sure i'll see what they say. i'll be over anyway. k. i'll be there soon.

wait, wait, lemme talk to him for a second. k, cal wants to talk to you. cal got the phone and walked onto the street. yo man, wut's good? i'm in a bit of a jam, gonna miss the last metro, do you think i can crash on your couch tonight? cheers man, thanks. word, ya mahn. so we see you soon then? sure. word. he went back over to the patio. cool, i can crash at edgar's tonight. ye? cool beans. he invited us all back over to smoke a spliff too. you guys wanna come? bobby looked to tina, it's on the way to your place anyhow. ya? okay. cool, we can share my pint and bounce, said cal. they passed the beer around, finished it quickly and left the bar. the streets were busy, it was thursday night. kids running about laughing, drunker than they. out of town businessmen leaving the strip clubs. the mcdonald's packed as usual.

bobby was on his toes. dwayne the dealer could be near, he probably was, or some of his cronies. he joked about it. if a thug muthafucka comes up and tries to start shit with me, just keep walkin. i've got some business to attend to. what kinda business do you have to deal with yo? lol. someone owes me. is that so? sure man, whatever you say. you can tell he's drunk when he starts thinkin people owe him something, cal whispered to maggie. he put his arm around maggie's waist.

the four of them walked two by two. what do you think you're doing? getting fresh. tina and bobby walked in front of the other two. cal kissed maggie. she didn't try and stop him. ten blocks later they arrived at edgar's. hey man. oy oy. this is maggie, you know tina. the apartment was lit with a tall lamp in the far corner and another over the laptop on the coffee table. what ya been up ta, asked cal. i had to finish reading this book for tomorrow. it's crazy how they cram an entire semester's worth of reading into five weeks during summer school. it's mental. sounds like you should of come out then. what are you readin? lolita. next week the crying of lot forty nine. pynchon. ya, then done for the summer. sweet.

    yo edgar allen poe, you got some beats? maggie and tina sat on the couch. ya man, the computer's right there. yeee. bobby was sniffing around. sensimilia, ohhh sennnsssiiimmiilliiiaaa? oh ya, sorry, i smoked it all, i invited you over for the last joint. what!? haha, but i ordered more. you smoked all that weed to yourself?! but where were you earlier, i tried callin…i waited outside for a while….haha, don't fret bobby boi, it's right here. fuck man, he laughs. here. ha. ha. funny guy man.

    so this is where edgar lives? what did you expect eh? i thought we'd show up and you'd open the door in a svelt smoking jacket, book cases, at least a real desk with one of those old green glass lamp shades. no no, i like to keep it real. laughs. your name's maggie right? didn't we have class together? last year, with mrs. oyden? ohhh ya, she smiled. that's right. what a joke that class was. i could always smell the gin off her. ya, i swear, one exam i probly should of gotten a thirty nine but she gave me a ninety three. i heard she killed herself not too long ago, i saw it up on the department bulletin board. really? oh my god, that's so sad. i wonder what her deal was. apparently her husband killed himself a few years ago. poor bastard, was probly just tired of her and tried to get away then she just followed him. tina gasped, bobby!? haha. ya it's mean, i know, sorry.

    are we going to smoke a joint or what? tina was getting impatient. whoa, whoa, easy does it my junkie queen. fiendin are we? junkie queen?! do you want to get laid tonight? who's the junkie anyway? i don't believe any of us are tina. bobby looked around the room. speak now or forever hold your peace. shut up! right, man, guys, i think i'm in love. he went over and kissed her and they scuffled in the corner of the couch. i'm already on it, cal asserted.

    the music played out of the laptop speakers: the sun is shining, the weather is sweet ya…cal lit the joint and started shuffling his body to the groove. to the rescue, here i am! he took the first puff. he pulled back the smoke into his body, the paper drew back and smeltered the crystally chronic. calvin suddenly sensed that from this moment on, the lighting of that joint, the ordinary same ol shit he'd done a thousand times before, would change his life forever. it wasn't the scientific facts of supposed brain cell loss, it wasn't the sadhus of pashupatinath in nepal projecting their astral bodies into the same stars he looked upon at night, it was something more, everything and nothing at once. he exhaled and grooved then passed the joint to edgar.

    he went over and started to dance in front of maggie, he held out his hand and she giggled. i want you to know that, here i stand! no, no, no no no. dancing a reggae shuffle, slow…

    bobby, tina and Maggie got ready to go after that. Bobby gestured behind the girls backs like he was goin to score both of them. ciao guys. door closed. there's a blanket on the couch man, see you tomorrow, i'm going to sleep. word g. thanks. edgar closed his bedroom door. calvin took the lamp off, stretched out on the couch. He got up to check his emails one more time. Nothing really. Back to the couch and he thought himself to sleep.

2
two fridays later

dishes clanging in the sink. the water running. an abrupt disturbance from sleep. no regard for those who sleep in. uhhh... what time is it? ten thirty? oh, he's awake? uh. calvin, i've got some things i'd like you to do for me today. i'm not even awake yet. it's ten thirty calvin. i just need a few things from the store. cal dragged himself off the couch. took the pillows from the floor and placed them back on the couch. folded up the hand knitted quilt. Okay, just let me wake up, please. he walked past the kitchen where his grandma finished washing the dishes. lazy, lazy, lazy she muttered, her voice trailed until cal closed the bathroom door behind him. he didn't take those remarks all to serious, she was just bustin his balls.

grandma wiped up the counter, went to rest her weary bones and sat down in her big arm chair. on the lamp table, beside the phone, she reached for her paper and pen. so what do i need? milk, o.j, bread, bananas are on sale, gino, a dozen eggs... cal walked out of the bathroom. grandma took forty dollars out of her wallet while cal sat on the couch and rolled a cigarette. are you working today? she asked. no, but starting tomorrow i'm goin to be full-time. ohhh, well that's good news. i guess it is eh? then you can take me out to dinner. sure thing. i think i get discounts at the high class restaurant, they have a book signed by all sorts of prime ministers, even bill gates, ya, the plates are expensive, you eat with silverware and everything. fancy, she said. you'll have to wear dress pants if you want to come with me. what?! he sputtered, almost not believing his ears. she laughed. right, so what do you need from the store. he got up and she handed him the list. can you get oatmeal, molasses and raisins too? it's not on the list, let me write it down. no, no, i'll remember. get yourself something if you want. cool, thanks g-ma. i'll be back then. he went to the closet and changed into his pants and threw a tee shirt on. he got his shoes, cigarette in his ear, hat on. out the door. he went out the back way as usual. he saw the broken table propped up by the dumpster...

cal decided he would try his hand at bingo yesterday in the golden isles rec. room. there were only eleven people there to play, thirteen when cal and his grandma joined. the group was an eclectic mix of older generations. some of them could barely understand what the others were saying. two women sat facing each other, speaking haïtian creole. the white québecoise were at ease discussing amongst themselves. when one of them would speak to grandma or mrs. edie, they wouldn't bother to slow down or articulate their words any less than what was natural to them. grandma or mrs. edie would respond accordingly, in english. this was enough for both parties, it was the way it had always been. whatever wasn't understood in words was generally conveyed in gesture and tone. whatever was lost probably couldn't of been that important. they also knew better than to ask anyone outside of their mother-tongue anything that would be too much of a burden to comprehend. but then, some of them were just playing the part.

the rec. room door mechanically opened and everyone looked to see who pressed the button. mr. baxter shuffled his way in the way those who really need a walker walk: step. by step. by step. oh god, said grandma, she leaned over to mrs. edie. what is he doing here? i thought he wasn't moving in till next week, mrs. edie replied. who's that? asked cal. mr. baxter. baxter baxter. baxter baxter? yes, baxter baxter. calvin snickered, talking quietly among his grandma and mrs. edie. what a name.

baxter baxter grew up in little burgundy back in the day. one of the tough guys, he fought his way to where he had to get to in life. a boxer, a drinker, he later worked in the train yards until he retired. he also knew cal's grandfather from rockhead's club. as some do in old age, others were looking on at baxter baxter with suspicion. his oxygen tank was attached to the walker so the most convenient spot for him to sit was at the end of a table. calvin sat at the end of a table, the spot across from him was free. grandma sat to calvin's left, mrs. edie to grandma's left. baxter baxter hauled himself over to the spot across from cal. all besides cal acted like they had absolutely no interest in acknowledging each others presence, it was like they were just too cool. looks like i got here just in time, said the old man, loud and proud. everyone looked at him again, his smile was wide, still voracious. how many cards would you like to play, baxter? i'll just take two, please and thank you, mrs. edie. baxter, this is my grandson, calvin. calvin, this is mr. baxter. he knew your grandfather. howdy, sir. no shit!? i'll be damned, and ya look just like him. who? ya granddaddy, son, he said stern. oh. baxter chuckled. you comin to spend time with your grandma? actually i'm stayin with her for a while. is that so? gettin some good home cookin eh boi? ye. did you go to school with my grandfather? you can say that. until i stopped goin, there was more money in winnin fights for me than to be readin all those books. i fought hard, son. you understand? uh huh. don't you uh huh me, junior. cal looked over to his grandma like, did he just say that? so you're moving in i hear, said grandma to baxter. that is correct.

okay, *on va commencer avec le bingo*! we will start the bingo, said the volunteer organizer. it was just pure luck, winning at bingo. cal hadn't been for a few weeks but it appeared, by the looks coming from mrs. leduc, she hadn't forgotten cal had won last time he was there. g52. ooo, off to a good start. i20. b14. n32. hello! oh, hehe, i said hello, not bingo. b6. g50. b5. b3. b11. n45. what street did you live on in burgs, cal asked baxter. i lived on every street in burgs. you go there now and people are still talkin about me. i lived on quesnel street for a while. oh ya? ye. you know little willie? joyce, you didn't teach this boy any respect? o65. my mama used to beat me for talkin the way you do to your elders. g58. b4. calvin looked over to his grandma's cards. b-i-g-o. oh snap grandma! o73. i29. you're tellin me, baxter started, you just livin off your grandmother here? no, i have a job. i went a while without any work, just getting back on my feet now. let me tell you somethin, when i was your age i had to feed two kids, take care of my first wife when she couldn't get no work cleanin homes in westmount. i had to pay rent. shit, son. i fought my way. we all did. ain't that right, joyce? n39. what are you talking about now baxter, leave the boy alone. n34. so close. ye, but...calvin started. hey, ya but nothin! you listen. you kids don't listen these days. baxter baxter wasn't even listening to the numbers being called. o63. we busted our asses for you kids. g56. that's somethin you don't think about. and your lazy ass doesn't give a damn about education, or work, or family. you just want the world to hand everything over to you.

n44. bingo! bingo! grandma cried. she read over her numbers to the arbiter. we have a winner! gagnant! everyone clapped and there was a general sense of communal good, clean fun in the room. since there was fourteen people playing grandma won 14 dollas. well, well, well, calvin said to grandma, look at you eh grandma. oh ho. grandma was excited. calvin, i have to go to the washroom, can you play my cards? sure thang, g-ma. i get 50% if you win though. hehehe, grandma snickered. she got up. i'll be back, she smiled to the arbiter. okay. *nouvelle jeux!* new game! calvin looked across to baxter. baxter looked at him and seemed to suddenly remember he was serving cal the morale. cal started before the old man got a chance. i don't need school to teach me how to read books. what do you have to show for yourself, son? b7. can i just have a second to explain? listen here, you might learn something, boi! calvin sighed. n35. ya, maybe i will, maybe i won't. what?! if you were only half as smart as your granddaddy i wouldn't be inclined to knock some sense into you. excuse me? this guy is too much, cal said out loud in mrs. edie's direction. she was too involved in bingo. what was that?! cal was trying to ignore the old man. n31. n39.he thinks he could beat me? ha. he'll be needin a whole lot more than his dialysis and air tank if....man. calm down mr. baxter. n32. boy, what do you have to say for yourself? you gotta be a man or the world will eat you up!

are you a man, son? cal looked around to see if his grandma was coming, mrs. edie was to involved in the game. you know what, i've gone to school, i go to work, like what? do you know? cal leaned in, like a fuckin slave, he whispered, sincerely. servin some 'massa' just like you did. ain't nothin changed, only now, they figured out i'm no good dead, lynched, so they keep me alive and suck the life out of me a little bit at a time. a fuckin slave. god save the motherfuckin queen. baxter looked at him and a spark of rage tweaked in his eye. why you little. baxter worked himself up to his feet. he began to look deranged. he raised his hands to box, wavering. you, uhhh, oh, oh! and he collapsed and fell right over the table. the legs of the table broke under him end and he tumbled down through the table to the floor. the game stopped and everyone gasped. 9-1-1. call 9-1-1! what happened?! *oh mon dieu! que-ce qui s'passe?!* calvin backed away from the table. the heap of mr.baxter tangled in the tubes of his air tank, lie immobile on the floor. bingo was over. mr. baxter died from a heart attack before the paramedics showed up. nobody blamed or suspected cal of anything.

☙

bobby was downtown busking near the eaton center. it was busy, even for a friday afternoon, which meant $$$ for the buskers, panhandlers, iced cream vendors and park kiosks. bobby had just sang broke again six times in a row and made about twenty seven bucks. not bad at all. like any artist, there's a pride buskers had in living off their art, even though most of them will never make the billboard charts, even though it was almost a daily, weekly, or monthly challenge to feed, drink, pay rent, and live just below modesty. as was also the case for bobby.

    he could never be on the street for long until he ran into someone he knew. he'd been busking for about thirty minutes now and decided to take a smoke break. who would the tide of pedestrian traffic bring up? none other than eely, a wirey, light of the lightest brown complexion chai children. what's up bobby? bobby low on his fold-out stool. what's happenin eely? just hustlin man, you know. where you off to. goin to work. hey, you know, they're holdin a walk-in interview session today. front and back house. full time and part time i think too. you should come by. bring a cv and shit, maybe shave. word, word. where's your restaurant again? on stanley street, between sherbrooke and maisonneuve. riiiight. ya man! sure, when's a good time to go? it's on all day, first come first serve. just tell the waitress and she'll bring you up to the office. dope! ya mahn, i'll go get myself cleaned up and get, get, get on over. word b. come through to the kitchen and say what's up, i'll be there. aright bro, thanks for the heads up. ya mahn. i could at least use some part time supplement. yo, there's a party tonight too, at herring's. you comin? i dunno, i didn't hear about it. i gotta work till close but ya, i'll try and swing by when i'm done. i gotta get goin though, i'm goin to be late. what time is it? Ten fifty five. aright man. check ya later. word. a+. eely walked back into the sea of traffic. the people kept on passing by, bobby packed up edgar's guitar into it's case. he swung it over his back, cig dangling from his mouth. he called up edgar to see if he was home so he could return the guitar and maybe grab a shower. there was no answer as bobby looked on, watching the people. shit. he began to slowly walk in contemplation then thought of calling mac. yooo, mac. what are you sayin? just thinkin right now. just sittin there thinkin eh? are you at home? sure am, pass by if you want. ok. cool man. see you soon.

    bobby got to mac's and knocked on the door. nobody came. he knocked again and tried the door knob. it was unlocked so he let himself in. the walls were covered in bits of paper:

pinned up
notes   drawings sketches   short poems magazine cut-outs
                                       newspaper poster articles

collages – it was like

entering the living space of a stalker or madman. he walked into the living room and found mac sitting and the table, face first on a blank sheet of white paper, writing onto another paper at the same time. mac? ya mahn, mac responded without taking his face off the paper. the phone beside him. what are you doin? you okay? ya mahn, it's an experiment. paralinguistics. metanarratives of the body used to extract carnal knowledge. like reading the future from the grains in an empty cup of coffee. or like palm reading.

   huh? a half hour a day, over a month, i hope to gather enough data from the dirt, oil and hair follicles so that, as my face ages and dusts, i can compare the body data to the poems i write at the same time in order to create a geodesic time capsule, made from the inside out, so that future generations can analyze the emotional resin of my bodily debris and poetic practice, praxis, in order to display the dance of my felt-sense in holographic form. what the hell would they do that for?! it's evolutionary! it would be a kind of teaching device, a diachronic unfolding of non-metrical, multi-dimensional systems. riiight. it's okay man, i just need ten more minutes. feel at home. cool g, don't mind if i grab a shower then? go right ahead. cheers. mac carried on.

   bobby was surprised to see how clean the bathroom was, although it was bare. he looked around for a razor. when he opened the medicine cabinet he found that razor, but also empty prescription bottles of haldol, clozapine, zyprexa. bobby noticed the milligram dosage increases. he also noticed they were dated from before bobby even knew mac. none of the took him by surprise and he began shaving.

      the
          syndetic
              erosion
                  of time
                      and time   space

                              and space   time

  turning through and through and through and through…

the marrow of
                              life

in the apartment was in constant transference --to-- quarter transference to half to 1/16 to 37.43 to all, constantly varying between everything else. mac's passion was above all else archaic but pure. the
gravity no. 1 of transference sifted cyclically, a truly bionic function of matter often ignored. he
gravity no. 2 wanted this. transference. he coped since his father's will enlisted him to purgatory. a
gravity no. 3 profit pressured parenthood, his father's passion handed down in pill form. you will help
gravity no. 4 save others as i try and save you. live through me, by me, i will be your saviour, you,
gravity no. 5 messiah, my son. mac's kundalini instinct waved and spun, swallowing, evading, then
gravity no. 6 accepting, even the smallest truth, or untruth, may be significant. not your bag? leave it
gravity no. 7 to someone else? but what do they know? feel? live, love and hate? the poison runs
gravity no. 8 in my blood, your cure and words light up my mind, brash and boiling, like a cauldron
gravity no. 9 brewed by bitches. the electric burned body that oozes filth they won't accept as good
gravity no. 0 enough – too far gone. we must bring him back. more! more! more! we're going to lose him, give him more!

forced into gluttony, realized in the antithesis of equality. sought out of all that shouldn't be, look on to the twinkle of his eye, childhood memories and aspirations to this brooding orb of the counter-linear tsunami you've ironically grown to fear. how? how?! luckily his instinct is strong, he intuits sanctuaries that found themselves long before continental reason took on the appropriation of eastern ways. and now that that's lucrative, the paranoia of its expropriation, back down to the underground, is your harrowing guilt. unseen, you are guilt. you've made it so for us all:// here comes that dandy they call reason (known as reason as rhetoric).

hark! will of the arc! covenant soul, what pains you? does the oasis of the sands of egypt not provide with water and shade in the afternoon sun? do you hoax mirages from aramaic translations to pacify? superstitious conniver, kneeling is all you suffer, upon sight of what is immaculate, behold, my scroll! in alexandria, port, abysinnians, sahara moselms, a norse warrior and the two dark children said to be from the end of the earth, taste my offering or be with the pharisees.

ah ha! yes, i knew it would happen! hark hark hark, your spirit was found up for auction. hark hark hark. one temple, two temple, three temple, four, she gave birth to you, that babylonian whore. after the second she did hear a new lesson, she destroyed all the temples, one temple, two temple, three temple, four. upon sight of what is great, revere my roman ideals of democracy. a member of the senate poisoned, back-corridor shanked...shanked!?!:// i may be simple but i suggest you just shut that face of yours. oh! hark hark guards guards! apprehend him! it's too late ya dandy. it's too late!

☙

bobby walked out of the bathroom, ain't nobody dope as me shamone so fresh, so fresh and so clean, clean. mac wasn't sitting at the table anymore. all that remained was a notebook, a pen, a stack of blank, white paper. on the floor beside the table was what appeared to be mac's dead dust poems, each paper labeled by date. will they be able to bring them back to life? is the dust even dead? so many questions, can't answer them all.

    mac? the bedroom door was open – nobody there. what the fuck eh? he'll probly be back soon. shamone, a printer. bobby logged onto the laptop laying on the couch. he checked his emails quick and downloaded his resume, printed it. at the same time he noticed neitzsche's geneology of morals in a stack of books. should probly read it. he got up and looked in the kitchen to find a bag. a reusable grocery bag. okay, let's get out of here. resume, check. book, check. i'll get the guitar later. out the door. won't lock it, he never does anyway, he'll probly be back soon.

    bobby was considerably excited about the prospect of a job. he enjoyed working in kitchens and learning new recipes. he voluntarily lost his last job when he asked his roommate at the time if he could replace him so he could go to a show. his roommate agreed and when bobby came home from the concert he found his roommate asleep on the couch. it was the second time bobby's replacement didn't work out, the first time he had asked mac.

    as he walked back downtown towards the restaurant he thought about the things he would do with his first pay. a guitar, definitely. a computer would be good, maybe enough money to get across the country? who knows? bobby walked in his world of thoughts until he heard a from behind him: yo! he turned around and saw dealer with another guy. you ready to pay? asked the dealer. shit. bobby took off running. you lie to me, you only lie to yourself bobby, yelled the dealer. they jumped into a car and followed bobby. they rolled up beside bobby as he kept running, where do you think you're goin to go, look at this hippie mother fucker, like he's at a fuckin track meet. pull up over here, dealer told the driver. bobby took a sudden turn down an alleyway. a fence at the end, fuck. he jumped it no problem just as dealer and his cronie ran down the alley after him. bobby looked back, his bag was light, zarathustra had fallen out while he jumped the fence. he still had his resume though. cot damn. he kept on running out the other end of the alley. dealer and his cronie didn't bother jumping the fence for two hundred bucks, it was just for amusement at this point.

    he was only a block away from the restaurant, he wanted to get off the street a.s.a.p. he kept running till he got to the front door of the restaurant. stopped, tried to compose himself, and entered. the restaurant was chic, black, white, glass, jazz, a waterfall. a pretty brunette with hot red lipstick and almond skin greeted him. bobby wiped the sweat from his forehead and let the air conditioning cool him off. hi there, said the girl. hi, i'm here for an interview. eely told me to come by. oh. okay. if you can just fill out this application and follow me. sure, thanks. bobby followed her up a wide plush carpeted stairway. there were a few more folks waiting. are you applying to the front or the back of the house, asked the girl. the back. okay, i'll let the chef know you're here, it shouldn't be long. thank you.

    he sat down and filled out the application. judging by the looks of the other people waiting, they were all applying for the front of the house, you could tell, they were all so fashionable. he looked around the room, at the old pictures of montréal, it appeared to be a restaurant with the same name. then a picture of that building burned down. some pictures with men standing together, autographed, he thought one guy might have been maurice 'the rocket' richard.

    then a big chef walked in the room, reading from resume in his hand. bobby? bobby jumped up, yes sir, that's me. how are you? he shook his hand. fine, thanks, the chef replied. we'll just go into my office over here. okay, have a seat, and the chef sat behind his desk. so, bobby, what position are you applying for? um, well eely told me to come by, i'm not sure what you guys are looking for, but i've done it all. bobby shook out his shirt for more air. do you find it hot in here. oh, no, not really, it's hot outside. i had to run before i got here. can you believe it, i got chased by some street thugs who were tryin to rob me, just while i was on my way here, but i got away. is that so, said the chef, skeptical and not impressed.

    i'm just lookin for some honest work, sir. i can do prep, i can work the line, i'll even do salad or dishwashing. okay, well we are looking for a prep cook and a line cook. how are your knife skills? pretty good, i mean, i can do julian, bruschettas, dice, nice and fine. i can do all the basics, although to be honest there's been times i've left the kitchen with both my thumbs bandaged up. he laughed. the chef smiled mildly amused.

    it says here you worked at la bohême. what kind of food did you make there. um, you know, bistro food. but fancy bistro food. bavettes, tartars, um...a bison burger. there were three different menus, ye, um...i can't remember it all. i'm good at learning fast though. why do you want to work with us, besides a pay cheque? well i love cooking, and kitchens, working in a team environment, you know, camaraderie and all that good stuff. okay. can i call le bohême for a reference? um. ya, but last i heard management changed and they fired like seventy five percent of the staff. really? the chef looked shocked. ya, they liked to party a bit too much i guess, he laughed. do you have any questions? no, i think that's it. when can i expect to hear back from you? by monday or tuesday, and if you didn't hear back from me, well, it didn't work out. okay, thanks very much. they shook hands. have a nice day. thank you for coming in. is eely working? yes, but he's busy. alright then, thanks.

 calvin was now on the metro. he didn't really have any plans for the afternoon. he thought he'd stop by and see his buddy, tobin. he was still three stops away from vendome and was trying to relay something to paper.

 what wasn't here does – failed this land so everyone was no one. intriguing for everyone to live past presently being. precepts. and only then an no one be someone so no one and everyone becomes someone – the best fail to ruin a collapse of unity from duality can't will other.

 at vendome. walk two blocks to tobin's. cal walked around the back of the building to yell at tobin's window. tobin! tobin?! he appeared at the window. cal, what's up man? what are you sayin, yo? wanna smoke a spliff? ya man, come on up. word...

 they sit down inside, tobin back at his computer desk. what are you sayin on this sunny, friday afternoon? it's a friday, ain't got shit to do. might as well get high. hell ye boi. i've just been playin online. edgar plays that too. do you have him on there. no, what's his user name? i dunno man, i never got into it. do you wanna roll? with pleasure. you mind if i check my emails? sure. calvin manned the keyboard and typed like he had a million times before. he boasted a word per minute count of 182. nothing. man, who the fuck publishes poetry? i mean, i know who publishes it, and ye, some of em are good, and i respect em, but some of em ain't shit. i like your poems, man. cheers man, that does mean more than they do. i've been tryin to do this as long as i've been writin. they don't like rap songs, the shit was a rap back in the day. im just tryin to figure it out. nobody even bothers getting back back to me. why don't you make a chap book? i could do it myself ye, but it's the principal, tobin, the principal. tobin puffed the joint then passed it to cal, here man, relax. i can't be fucked anyway. cheers.

    tobin's place was kinda dingy, the smell of a million joints smoked and rotted. unlike mac's place, tobin rarely cleaned, especially the bathroom. the bathtub was so dirty there were rings around it just from showering. but he was a good friend of cal's, and he was always down for a joint. that might be his downfall, he was on the upper end of what can be considered a non-functional pothead.

    ya see, there are two kinds of potheads, the functional and the non-functional. tobin could be considered on the upper end of non-functional because it was probly true that the weed didn't mix well with his anti-psychotic medication he got administered during his visits to the douglas hospital. he had experienced a hebephrenic psychotic surge following the year after high school. it may have been the joints which he could of taken a break from, it may have been the other meds he was served by the psychiatrist he saw after his episode, either way, it's been years now and besides having succumbed to his atypical psychotic behaviour and phobias, he was just a normal guy that smoked weed and played video games, he went through some shit, a period of extreme sensitivity. was he frozen? immobile in his world, complacent, or did they tell him that's the safest way. he's never been too far gone, he just needed a few months off the joints, not a regular doses of injections over a lifetime. but who's to say, the doctors know best, right?

    but don't pharmaceutical companies need to try out their new products? don't they need to sell enough to at least break even from the cost of production? don't they want more than just breaking even so they can be

                         wealthy?
                  wealthy to consume,
     who will consume?   hetero-trophic **organisms**
                                   are hungry: are after you
be
heterotrophic
monkey see and   simulacra   do   simulating acres
                    consume
        what i fear will consume me?
               consume out of fear.   **consumption**
                      is the progressive wasting of
              body tissue? i consume
               nothing but fear itself.

consume the fear and consummate with this dope for example. is your language fully digested?

     back to the earth we go, from the earth we grow?

died in fear of life, there's something wrong: with. you.
                             what is it that you fear?
                             nightmare's and murder
                mac and his **psycho mother**-tongue

really? oh my! well take this and when you no longer fear that that you fear you will be well, you will be free. i am here to help, *i will cure your design*. i have the will of **new** experimental drugs which have **proven effective** in clinical trials but have yet to be diagnosed in the long run. the effects are affects and we *love* you so. *don't we?* **oh yes we do**, *couchie, couchie, coo://*

i'm tired of this clown. chuckles. get down off that crown. gimme that crown! chuckles. chuckles threw the crown up into fractal oblivion and said, here, catch, keep doin your thing you done did and done do: may induce night terrors, diarrhea, migraines, nausea, loss of mobility and an overall feeling of no well-being. can't stop, won't stop mutha fucka, get dooowwwnnnn baby, or lay doooowwwnnnnnn baby.

    you wanna go to this book launch tonight? uh, i dunno, jerry was supposed to come over and play starcraft. you goin to be missin out, well, i mean, he'll be readin some of his new stuff, answerin questions. i just wanna hear what he has to say. who is it? don walynpio. ya, i don't think so man. word, what time is it? you wanna grap somethin to eat? sure, i'm starvin. they decided on goin to capoli's, where the burgers are so big they could feed a family. the rest of the late breezy summer afternoon was spent smokin joints, and listenin to oldies and hip hop on youtube. tobin wasn't prone to drinking so cal figured he'd walk from vendôme to downtown and grab a beer before heading to the launch. although there'll probly be someone at the launch selling st.ambroise for two bucks out of the case.

∽

they had met once, in a bar, cal recognized his face. hey sir, how are ya. my name's cal, i've been readin your poetry. when he went to shake walynpio's hand he forgot to be formal and tried to shake his hand like a brotha. the moment walynpio couldn't follow the hand shake he got nervous and looked embarrassed and said, oh, ho, i'm too white for that stuff. oh, haha, that's alirght. and walynpio walked off with this friends in the other direction. he may be too white to shake a hand like a brotha but that don't mean he can't be one. anyhow, it looked like he was getting ready to speak. the room had filled up quite a bit, some older folks were there too, more writer types, or professors. he got in front of the room and tapped on the mic. hello. he tested. well, i'm not so happy to see so many familiar faces, because that means you think i'm doing something right, which means we're all in trouble. the room laughed on cue. thank you, both familiar and unfamiliar faces for coming out to the launch of my new book, there was no winner. i'll read a few poems, then we'll hear my great friend, peter mclusky, read from his governor general nominated book of poetry. then we can proceed with the drinking. sound good? they all cheered.and indeed there was, where don walynpio's new book of poetry entitled, there was no winner, was on sale for a modest enough to be vain total of $20.00. they call it a sale? walynpio was talking to two attractive young girls. he was a creative writing professor, they were probably his students. there were a few little groups of younger, student type folk, scattered around the room, sittin in chairs, standing by the concession stand sippin on beer, outside smokin cigs. the level of jittery excitement in the room was nauseating, giddy and naive. was it like this all the time? these people, creative writer types. and they were all here to buy, or at least support, their teacher's new book like one big bukakke circle? chuckles. naw, but it ain't that bad, let em write and learn. aspirations and all. see who can listen.

    cal went to sit down then got back up and walked over to the concession stand. he stood beside the two talking to the vendor. the vendor looked at him then looked back at the two while they finished their anecdote.

    so we were hitch-hiking and i had a b.b. gun in my duffle bag, and someone must of seen the gun when i opened my bag for a minute cuz when we got off the ferry and took a nap in the shade the cops woke us up and said we were under arrest. do you have a gun they asked. i said a b.b. gun. then they looked in the bag and called off back-up. ridiculous really. they all laughed. calvin was getting annoyed he was being ignored. hi, the vendor said, ever so sweetly, how could he be angry at such a pretty girl?

    hey, how much are the books? twenty bucks for the new one. calvin exhaled and looked over to walynpio. okay. i'll buy a book and a beer, please. that'll be twenty five dollars. what? how much is the beer? two dollars. there's tax on the book. tax? yes, tax. but not on the beer. cal exhaled again and forked over the twenty five bucks. here you are. thanks, and he went back and sat down. there was no winner. cal flipped the book open, periodically lookin up to see if walynpio was free. calvin had sent him a few emails, askin him questions and opinions about the last book of poetry he had written. cal thought it to be imperative he knew what this man thought. he shamelessly admired walynpio's work, he didn't care tryin to act otherwise, he also didn't care to pay to learn by supporting that knowledge vault and debt and those interested in interests.

insert poems into space and time: fractal usurper: appropriation, expropriation, repropriation, depropriation.

everyone applauded and walynpio introduced mclusky. walynpio sat on the middle of all the chairs for the entire remainder of the reading. cal couldn't get to him yet. meanwhile mclusky, morose and half drunk, sending eye flirts to one of his female students, driving her crazy like she was under the spell of an old fat jim morrison, read his poems. how did he get nominated? can barely call it innovation. he's pissed off at the snow queen, i'm pissed off at him, he can't think of any better fairy tales. there's no winner. if all it takes is a few essays by his former students to justify and appreciate his sublime ham and cheese sandwiches then shit, call me grey owl and get me lynched by pissed off xenophobes.

after a few comedic and imaginative poems there was a line-up of people at the concession stand waiting to buy the new book, or hey, a book and a beer! 25 dolla! get your book and a beer! 25 dolla! cal was tryin to remember exactly what he wrote to walynpio in his last two emails over the last two months. he was now at the front of the line. hi mr. walynpio. cal gestured the handing-over of the book to be signed. it's not mister, walynpio said sarcastically. do you remember we met at korova once, i introduced myself to you. walynpio peered up at him, queer and squinting. i've emailed you a few times about your last book. oh ya, what's your name again? cal. right. did you get my emails? right right, you wanna be a writer right? well i suggest you become a teacher. here ya go, thanks for coming out kid! and he handed him back the book, signed. it read, keep on losing! don walynpio. cal kinda just automatically moved out the line of bodies flowing behind him so they could have their own turn to see walynpio. he walked out of the store. nothin would settle, the dust just stayed dust and there was that cloud, a merky fog.

    i should become a teacher? a teacher? i have to write, what glorious? indentured professionalism? owe, to what, to who, debt to the institution that bricked me or civic duty to give to the people, the world that inspires. i don't even know what i ask, i don't know why i ask, but i can't care.

        the insatiable appetite of a rabid dog lurking home
cal made his way, he had to work tomorrow morning, already, deep
in the   porous
           crust of
               what could become sediment. but not yet.
               sediment.said.i.meant
               work tomorrow?
there's work to be done today
                    (if he survives today's) forget about
                        tomorrow.
               i am my nigger
                   -gonna have to serve somebody
no shame
no pride
i won't be exchanged in that economy.

twenty six letters a b c d e f g h i j k l m n o p q r s t u v w x y z &
      - what happened to the 27th continuum?

old thinking alphabet.
the new and old alphabet,
which is older   will the new one think too?
                       will it think like me?

                                                    will i become?
                    meet   obsolete – *the* data cannibal
                                                   take me if you can,
like the natural selection   skeleton   eat me whole, let me rot
                                            your insides, cook me well,
                            you can't get it out
                                          i've already **been**

boiled, smoked, burned, sauteed, baked, basted, fried,

you still can't get rid of that taste, my flesh that denies you a good night sleep. at the base of it all, you **can't**   dutifully deny me, or replace me with novelty, for:ever.

won't   outside the castle walls are the *myths* and **warnings** you heard as a child. don't wander the **will**   streets at night, alone, in the forest, among the wolves, a creed seethes in its folly, unquestioned, **why**   undefined totalities i know because they are not i. ah, but for **i**, *you*, outsmart, **you,**
don't outsourcing   the reaches of my tongue

tastesthatdazzleand*ration*reasontotherhetoricaltipofafinallyhoned*blade*icallagu*ri*callthe*law*icalledan
                                     apo
                                                            -logy.

            jesus?
                      disciples   socrates?
                                                            pupils

cal got to his grandma's apartment and took of his shoes. in the closet was his duffle bag, he had the last few swigs of a mickey of whiskey which he grabbed and took outside to sit down with on the balcony. he lit a smoke and kept on.

everything couldn't be so, i know, i know, the world, would it be dark or light? if absolute took over? but am i damned, doomed, decrepit, deemed, dubbed in perpetual dawn, dusk? but then again, i can't care. i employ, implore and conceive.

>   moving with:in.
>   moving with:out.
>   moving in:with.
>   moving out:with.

cal tried to watch a movie but he was too displaced to pay attention. old westerns, call girls, an elvis movie, news, news, olds, shopping channel, i can do this forever, he thought, a television continuum. no, a circuit continuum like a rolodex codex, xxx, how bout maggie? i never got her number. might as well see if i can again. if i see her, and tina, well, i won't bother askin her about her. with dick in hand he gradually drifted to sleep watching the call girl infomercials.

 he opened his eyes. you gotta be kiddin me? print it! you think i'm fuckin kiddin you? you think i'm fuckin kiddin you?! how's this for a joke. gun. you're goin to give me an advance. i was going to get back to you soon. blank stare. did you read it? he didn't reply quick enough. you're takin the piss outta me. i'm tired of this shit. i've been patient. i am patient. you'll understand, maybe even be, well, you'll be thankful. this is bigger than you and me. you know how this shit works. we fuckin live this shit. time's brought us here, the both of us, it could have been anyone else, but it's us. you're out of your mind. huh, ha, yeah, sometimes i wish i was. what do you think you're doin? calling the police. unbelievable. he picks up the phone and throws it across the room. the phone smashes the frame hanging on the wall.

 can we be serious for a minute? just settle down. are you okay? i mean… he noticed calvin change after he asked him. calvin noticed he noticed. the timbre changed auburn to silver blue. the editor sat behind his desk on the edge of the chair, poised in effort to hide the anxiety coursing between them.

 calvin started looking around the office. piles of boxes filled with books to be sold and shipped off. he bolted to the window and threw a glance over to the editor, looked out of the 3rd story window then shut it.

    print it! you're not goin to play some fuckin negotiator, there is no negotiation. i've got a plans, b plans, c plans, hell i got enough plans to write an alphabet. print the contract! you're not going to use that gun. are you fuckin questionin me? the man with the gun? the anxiety was climbing up calvin's back. it began to overwhelm the original adrenaline rush.

    god damnit! calvin shot a round into the floor with his cheap black revolver. from this point on he now knew nothing more than his own delirium, and the editor finally realized it too. it was eight thirty on a saturday night and there was nobody in the entire building. how bout i give you a break? yeah, i think you deserve a long weekend. i'll make sure you don't have to come in on monday either. yeah, that sounds good. i'll make sure to tell stacey too. what? how? forget about it. print it now, i'll walk out of here once i sign that dotted line and you sign your name on a cheque. the sooner the better. after that i'll make a phone call to tell some guys they don't need to go to 2025 redpath anymore. if you go near her i'll...save it! i don't need to hear that shit, this is real life, you're not goin to be a hero and i'm not goin to be the bad guy. calvin tilted up his chin and thought: and i'm not goin to be a hero and you don't have to be the bad guy either. this is a new world, a new time. how could you not give a fuck?

    i admire your devotion.

    i've heard that before, admiration, devotion, but those words...why does it always come back to words? right, go on, tell me something, fix this! fix the words! where's the music?! i'll talk...what's the password? calvin points the gun at the editor. put your hands up. get out of the chair. enough talk. move! okay okay. empty your pockets. put everythin on the desk. slowly. calvin stood with the revolver at his waistline, constantly pointed at the editor. he was at one end of the desk and the editor stood at the other. back up! lie on the floor with your palms down where i can see them. he sorted through the contents of the editors pockets on the desk. i'll take that money now, i'm kinda hungry. and a cellphone. he picked up the cellphone while quickly and constantly looking back over to the editor. he looked through the call history and text messages.

    you little fuckin cunt. he shot into the floor. the editor shuttered and turned his face away, cheek on the floor. you really fucked this up didn't you? i can't even be fucked. then the cell rang. huh, looks like its your mom callin you…how sweet. let me talk to her. how sweet. let me talk to her! give me the phone! do you fear your mother? what? please, i'm…no! alright! i run the show, i call the shots, i'm the fuckin man! i don't know who you texted but you and i, we're getting out of her now. stand. get on your feet. come on!

    calvin took one step towards the editor then the door splintered and cracked. within an instant the room was full with a swat team of six officers in helmets and holding rifles. there's no way they could of gotten here that fast. freeze! put down the gun! put the gun down. nobody needs to get hurt. calvin's eyes, ice, crystalline, staring into the reflective glare of the officer's helmet visor. he couldn't will himself to stop, a paralysis. he raised the pistol to shoot himself in the head, quickly and robotic. before he raised the revolver to his temple the swat team unloaded on him, they wouldn't even let calvin off himself.

and then there was a party

bobby, mac and isabelle were all hangin, pre-drinkin at edgars. they'd been at it for about an hour now, although mac wasn't drinkin. bobby was intermittently pre-occupied with youtube dj duties, isabelle was giggly and forthwith, leering with her eyes, adding to the guise of collective inebriation with her broken franglaise. edgar was rollin another joint and mac held a guitar, cross legged on the floor, riffin off what bobby played.

    yo, what time is it, asked edgar. nine thirty, you guys wanna leave soon? i just want to finish my wine first, said isabelle exhaling cigarette smoke. ok. ye, i'm about done this forty anyhow, gonna have to restock before the party. is anybody down to get a bottle? of what? i dunno, whiskey. eeewww, no, she said. i got beer already. mac? i don't drink anymore. but if you quit, that means you can drink again. only wine or cider, once and a while. and he took a sip from isabelle's glass. bobby got up from the computer, lost his balance but quickly regained his balance. oh ho ho, mac noticed. ho ho ho santa clause. edgar passed the joint to bobby. isabelle went to the computer. can i play something? be my guest said bobby, or be edgar's guest. she was attractive, her eyes really incensed curiosity, her accent and artist allure. she was now on facebook but stopped the song. the eclipse is on wednesday. the abandonment, the downfall, the darkening. cease to exist. then isabelle's new song started. serge gainsbourg, dieux il aime les havanes. that's the greek meaning of the word eclipse. scary eh?

isabelle got up and bobby passed the joint to her as she began waltzing around the room. she half expected bobby to dance with her. but bobby was triggered and started freestylin over the song:

an ecliptic gimmick bringin the end of existence / to the tongue eclectic, it's all about the witness / what is this?...

oui, c'est quoi ca?! isabelle put the volume up on the computer. i want to listen to serge gainsbourg. you cannot control all the sound in the room like a fascist! ok there isabelle, let's not get too carried away. non! don't tell me what i am to do! i am a woman, you men will not....putain! fascho! mac got up, come on baby, he's not tellin you what to do. she's getting all riled up inside. québecoise vs. anglophone, woman vs. man, separatism, feminism, she was growin cold fangs for bobby...

come on now baby, we're all friends here. she was welling up inside, eyes watering, she got too drunk too quick, maybe it was the weed. functional vs. non-functional. actions and ideas of some inner discontent. i'm sorry isabelle. bobby apologised. although he didn't know what for.

i'm sorry i lied, i'm sorry i hurt you. i'm sorry for killing. stealing. thinking. fucking. wronging. righting. rape. kidnap. extortion. i'm sorry mother. i'm sorry sister. i'm sorry brother. i'm sorry father zossima. if we were all sorry then it'd be utopia. everyone can't be sorry for history. absolve! repent! ask jesus, the power comes from within. sorry for bumping into you, getting drunk, scruffing your shoes, denting your car, inciting hate for me for you for us. absolve! i forgive myself and you do the same. you can't take it all upon yourself. do something about it. you can't do anything, they're, dead! you can't do anything without fuckin it up anymore. you fucked up. you done fucked up son...

sorry for war. sorry for famine. i care, here i am, let me help. let us forget? i can forgive but cannot forget. i'll be good, gooder. let's learn from our mistakes. let's move on, move off, move we must, move we will, let's make it better, should i be ready to forgive you for the future, should you forgive me for the future? anticipation, it can kill. so i'll prepare my tombstone, plot my grave, would you like me to dig you one too? oh, no, i don't wish you'd die, i just wonder how far you will die? i'll give you me, voluntarily, i volunteer, i submit. you have been, or have you not been? i thought you were? is there something you're not tellin me?

babe, isabelle. lache moi! the situation was getting volatile, nobody really understood what was going on. mac backed up, bobby actually seemed frightened, edgar got up and picked up the joint that isabelle had thrown into the corner of the room. bobby looked at mac like what did i do? mac was bothered. *je ne veut pas être ici!* what's wrong? *je veut être chez moi, je veut partir.* okay baby, we'll go back to my place. *non! laisse moi, je veut être chez moi!* okay, let's go. the other two were still, watching, bobby stupified, edgar was rather amused by it all, casually puffing the joint. he passed it to bobby. isabelle bolted out of the apartment. mac froze and didn't know what to do for a second. he ran after her. isabelle! wait! the sound of the stained glass doorway shaking. bobby and edgar both walked over to the window and watched mac catch up to isabelle down the street. they disappeared out

of sight.
     what, the fuck, was that? i have no idea. pms? i dunno, i've never seen them argue before. that wasn't even an argument. she just exploded, maybe she was savin it for a rainy day. you pissed her off. man! i didn't do shit. well, anyhow, i'll finish her wine for her. maybe they'll come back. she said she wanted to go home. edgar stood at the window inhalin the last of the roach and threw it out the window. bobby slugged back rest of the bottle. yuuuugghhcckkk, i hate warm rose. can i use that bag you got for my beers? ya mahn. se we ready to roll then? i'm just goin to take a piss. bobby lit a cig and sat down at the computer one last time. window: email: window: youtube: window: facebook: status update: party at herring's tonite: log out: close window: edgar was still in the bathroom: combing his hair, brushing his teeth, cologne. come on man, what are you doin, puttin on your makeup? shamone! ya ya, chill out. i'm getting fresh for the ladies. don't fuck with my style. oh ho ha, okay man, okay. bobby grabbed a book and flipped through some pages. panopticon. okay, let's bounce then. shiiit boi, look at you. are we goin to the same party? his dress shirt was tucked in, hair slicked back, a regular christian bale.
     they walked out the apartment building and turned through the back alley shortcut. do you have a smoke for me? sure buddy. k, i'm just goin to run into the dep and pick up a bottle: open the sliding fridge door: ten dollar bill on counter: cash register open: change: outside. i only got like five bucks left on me. i'm goin to jump the metro: okay: i'll go first, no, you go first, buy a ticket, i'll jump then. word. word is bond yo: jump toll while edgar pays at the booth. it's only the young and athletic toll booth employees that'll sometimes chase you. better just hope there's no metro cops around. nice and cushy in their unionized toll booths. won't risk a confrontation for a three dollar fare. bobby waited at the far end of the landing, cracked open his 10% 40: people were everywhere, it was friday night. edgar and bobby got on the metro-car. laughing.time bending. which stop we getting off at? st. henri. then we getting off on some broads. hahaha.

yeeee boi. pound knuckles. slug back on the 40. already there.

   they walked out of the metro and took that darker back road beside the train tracks. man, you got two bucks you can lend me? i'm goin to buy another 40, this ain't gonna be enough to last me the whole night. you're going to be shitfaced any minute man, you can have some of my beer if you need. there'll be booze there too. ahhh, fine, edge, fine, edgar knows right, doesn't he? maybe he does? bobby stopped to piss on a car, fuckin mercedes benz mother fucker. you gotta make sure you piss all over the door handle, like so. what are you doing? you're crazy. poetic justice my friend. how many people do you think the owner of this car has pissed on. edgar walked around the car and onto the road. judging by the baby seat in the back...the baby seat makes it all that much better, we must infect their children too, or they will grow to avenge their forefathers, and their father's fathers before them. come on man, we're almost there. they multiply and we divide, the seas will part only when i am drunk enough.

   they kept on walking. edgar was being a light weight and cracked open a beer as bobby swung about with the forty in his hand. and what the fuck was that shit with mac and isabelle? i dunno, she probly wants to separate or somethin, i didn't do anythin is all i know. this land was stolen, can you take what's already been had? recycling land and people like ideas? it just sounds wrong. it's a matter of principle! fuckin hypocrites. decolonize or liquidate and die.

   the place looks packed. they turned off st. marguerite and saw all the people in the loft window on the other side of the canal:cross foot bridge over canal:enter big ol what-used-to-be-a-factory and climb what-always-for-some-reason-winded-you three story flight of stairs. they opened the door to the third floor, the music coming from the loft flooded the silence of the stairwell. they both smiled and concurred, knowin that it was goin to be lively. pumpin! shit boi, they walked down the huge hollow industrial corridor and stepped through the red door. people were everywhere. the projector playing natural born killers on the wall in the dimension of at least fifteen by twenty feet. boomba! you wuddup guys! out of the crowd emerged blais. yo blais, wuddup man, this place is bangin! ain't it! girls everywhere. one thing that was sure when herring threw a party. blais' roommate stevie was the mack of st. henri. she got more pussy than anyone. bi or gay, she got em all. probly even converted a few along the way.

so many people. bobby was doin the drunk dance. between edgar and blais: he's already more than half way in the bag. hey hey hey, bobby was getting down, contortin his face in an effortless craze. bobby boi! someone called. get over here. huh? he looked up and recognized. someone signaled him into the bathroom. mmm? he crooked his attention, he couldn't save himself and on he went. edgar watched him walk off, well that should straighten him up a bit.

the party was full of the bike-type punks, some hipsters, but everyone was being called a hipster these days. pretty girls of the acquaintance type that came out on the weekends for the parties. people were dancing, talking, making out, smoking cigarettes, joints, snortin coke in the bathroom, fucking in the bedroom, your usual bedlam and hedonism. the orgy.

mac had convinced isabelle to come back to his place. she lived on the other end of town, it was too far. candles were lit, incense. the comforter was pushed off the bottom corner of the bed by the grind of footing pushing. it was everything. sex medicine like beating drums, tribe and ancient and cleansing and restorative, dissolving sense. she wasn't angry anymore, she was good for him as he for her. he wasn't bewildered any more.
the practice, yogis. their minds a barren paradise of desert that only they managed to survive in. somehow, deep down, in the springs, tapped wells. they both surrendered to each others inferiorities cast by their shadows. everyone indulged. the simultaneity of disillusion, the simulation, the act, the event of horizon proliferating, scorching all, in one sweeping tide of astral projections teeming out from under the skin. relay. pull. the umbra force approaching was consistent like pagan definitions of blood and moon and moons. ra. yoruba. canaanite libation for the future from the past by the present by the future for the past

without the present from the present to nyama—chi.

in the dandy's court

translate, translate, oh you divine creature. i invite, come one, come all, come to my court and witness the oddities only i entertain. from the furthest reaches of constellations both torn and axenic. and look, the re-virgin, pure by devotion. story teller. please recant.

in a time that never is, a place that always was, health and sickness coincided. it might have been a chaste marriage, an age of asherah reterritorialized and introduced to the 21st century, all that she was, from arabia, egypt to israel, had syncretically eloped in a litter of seventy offspring. josiah denied the seventy offspring and vanquished her from solomon's temples built for yahweh. today, josiah is an athiest who resides along the tracts of osmosis which govern the mitochondria, but before, in a book, his reality wasn't as capable of vengeance.

anyway, asherah was a protector, and as the mistress of both sea and land she may have been considered a bit too busy, a bit of a slut in some standards. the origin of slut shaming. and king asa's mother no doubt understood that in order to care for the land, asherah would have to be able to care for the sea as well, there couldn't be one without the other. if it was possible for asa to have defeated zerah, the kushite, by divine intervention, then it would be true that asherah wasn't called upon, but the question remains, did yahweh intervene by helping asa because asherah was being held captive for a ransom of divine intervention and the only way yahweh could have her back was by helping asa defeat zerah and send him back through egypt to the ethiop land of kush? (it should be noted that through menelik, asherah's descendant, that asa and zerah were probly third cousins and didn't even know it).

it is probly unquestionably so that yahweh loved asherah beyond compare, i mean, who wouldn't love an eternal protector? how could the legislators, the kinds of judah, have no consideration for their god's wife? was it enough for god to love only people? or did they think that she didn't have the time, that she was too busy with the land and the sea and in some auto-erotic affectation they scribed her as a whore then burned the documents and smashed her statues. did they try to convince god that he was better off without her? did god accept the loss of his love like a widower who could never replace that one special girl? boy did he ever get pissed off sometimes. he couldn't give two shits about the ones who took his lover away from him. he let it all go: wars, death, natural disasters, you name it, he said "deal with it yourselves".

every now and then, like he did with asa, he would intervene and help out, they thought he helped because they were pious, only the fools considered that god was reminding them of the pact of redemption, to which man never did keep his word. they irreverently ignored the considerate fools, discredited their oracular voices, their poesis of reason, for no true reason could ever be objectless or incalculable, they said. they said, well look here, the son of god, a jew, proves that god never needed asherah. ah ha, but wouldn't it also be the greatest love story of all time if the son of god was indeed the son of asherah? how could he, god that is, have a son without a lover? yahweh found asherah, and asherah yahweh, and they consummated in exile to propose an illegitimate son as a symbol of sacrifice to man for choosing to keep yahweh and asherah separate, because the godly couple knew it wasn't right to keep them apart. because they loved people (maybe asherah more than yahweh), this son died for all of our sins, but primarily for insisting that god could have no wife if he was to be a god of man, or so they promote. and so from the exile of babylon on, when nationalism was elected by patriarchy as a symbol of the strength needed to align the people under one rule and law and never to be weak again, asherah herself was forced back into exile and yahweh was practically enslaved until he himself would resign. they swore each others chastity until they would be free to love again.

those who believed they were pious to their celibate and lonely god asked him for health, wealth and wisdom. anyone who asked or thought about asherah was struck as being ill in the head, body or soul and was either forever relieved of their illness by death or enslaved to purgatory's poking and prodding encomienda of experimentations, exploitations like plantations. some say asherah whispers to them from exile, luring them away with her, along into a marginal universe, left forever to wander nothingness, left with whatever else was discarded and deemed non-functional, negatory, or if one were to dare say—evil.

sigmund freud, the infidel jew, considered the positive in the negative, the good in the evil, and concluded that you had to know the object in order to claim anything about it.

how well did josiah know asherah? how could he just assume she had no place in yahweh's temple? how could he articulate speech acts of value by smashing every trace of asherah off the ends of the earth? didn't milton consider hell's heroes? but he didn't consider it's heroines. questions into situations or situations into question. that would be rhetorical. no. hermeneutic. i end this parable like this: asherah was punished for her virtues, forgiven for her mistakes, which were sufficient enough grounds to get rid of her. yes, for after that, josiah thought he would be freer, but for what? tapped by a sinister metabolism, the mitochondria of josiah, could be the descendant-like proteins of asherah's seventy offspring—according to darwin.

bravo! bravo! i was drawn to tears, i found my pride, my kinship, wonderful, oh wonder. another story storyteller, we want an...the palace is shaking?! what in the? guards! what is happening? council, gather the council! i fear the time has come! was it not supposed to last!? storyteller! what have you done, you will pay for this...oh my, how taxing this is! story teller!

friendly foe

what's your problem man? bobby was all fucked up and starting trouble. this cunt's getting out of line, he told blais. you're a fuckin poser, bobby. posin opposer, bobby slurred and swung at blais and edgar's long time friend, franco. you're a degenerate piece of shit is what you are. who, hey hey. blais and edgar held bobby back. blais, what's this homeless fuck doin here? you can't even hold your liquor, tough guy eh. franco smashed bobby's face with two punches. franco, what the fuck are you doing? bobby was let free and lunged at franco. he tripped and fell and franco got on top of him and started feeding him shots. commotion broke out. stop it! yelled a girl. get him off of him. edgar pulled franco off of bobby. bobby, bloodied and out of breath gathered himself to his feet.

    fuck this shit. the music still pumpin. Fuckin cunts! he stumbled past everyone and left the party. should someone go see if he's okay? he'll be fine, i've seen him in worse shape than that. he goes looking for it sometimes, trying to prove something or impress someone, mostly to himself. he enjoys the melodrama. it'll be a story he can tell until the swelling goes down and the cuts disappear. he laughs it off the next day. crazy bastard, he's lucky i didn't fuckin destroy him. fuck you franco, you threw the cheap shot. it was over nothing, franco, and you know that. well i don't want him coming back, said stevie, so you can beat him up if you want.

    someone should go see if he's okay though, said rebecca again. ya, you're right, edgar agreed. i'll go see if i can find him. i'll come with you if you want, said rebecca. sure, i don't think he's that far. unless he's wandering around the building. i'll just call him first. no answer. fuck. blais looked out the window. i see him. he's over there. ah, okay. he's a big boy, he'll be fine.

    rebecca knew edgar and bobby from the bar. she was one of those pretty girls that was nice and non-judgmental. geesh, it's been a weird night. first we were over at my hosue, before we came here, when all of the sudden out friend's girlfriend freaked out after she called bobby a fascist for controlling the music being played. then bobby starts up and storms out. i dunno what's goin on. that is weird. bobby's always been a sweet guy when i've seen him, even when he's drunk. he acts like he's okay and everything's cool but i think he's going through a bit of a rough patch. i mean he sleeps outside (but says it's better than paying rent), he lost his job a few months ago (but always manages to stay just above being absolutely broke), i dunno. ya, that's just the way his is, that's why we love him. i don't know how he manages to be so relaxed and happy (most of the time): self-medicated, self-depricated, self-educated. social disorder or social distorter? greek cynic.

  the age old game had begun between edgar and rebecca. do you wanna smoke a joint? naw, that's fine thanks, i don't smoke, it get's me all crazy, in my thoughts i mean. ye, i went through that before, in high school it made me dumb, then lazy and paranoid, now i just kick back and enjoy, i had to smoke my way to where i am today. she laughed. she knew he was in university , and look at the boy, as fresh as he was, a good advocate for the people who thought they were too white to listen to anyone else.

                one – we have lift off
                  two
                 three
                four
                five
               six
               seven
delta-nine-tetrahydrocannibinal eight

a few noses
sniffed the air
and
looked over to edgar.

                this is a contact high.
                just look.

                                              ya may think
it's dumb. ya may
feel dumb. ya could
be numb.   para.noid?   ya won't lose yourself
forever,
nuh uh, no way.

don't fall   through
               the hole
               the slit of the s   the space between
                    the l   the
                    the i   space-between
                    the t

                    sometimes
               if you listen real quiet,
                    real good like
                 you hear the silence.
                    sshhhh————————you hear that silence?

                         it
                    ain't as sneaky
                  as you think it is.
          it's the kinda silence that might make the folks
                 jump or scream like in a cinema,
                  but it ain't meanin to scare ya.
          naw, cuz it's that same silence you look for when.
               it's like. you how. i why. they what. we
                where. where we. what they. why i. how

                         you. like it.
                         when like. like
                         when. as how.
                              how as.
                              as why.
                              why as.

> like what.
> what like.
> where as.
> as where...tear me together.

cure my good. faithful in faithlessness. faithless in hope. foolish wisdom of the wise fool. of the of. find the found. found the find. these are _____. lost the lose. trip the trope. skip a **cope**. plan a can. wam bam thank you ma'am. tick for tack for tock. clock the space. space the clock. time the room. room the time in a **cell** powered by the sun of a **thermodynamic** panel. pass the past. refute the future. president of the present...naw. right of the wrong. wrong of the right. left of a right angle. rhetoric read or is. sick or sober. trick a clover. pickin's over. never. royal borer. nomadic borrower.
burrower. borougher.
sorrower or sojourner truth.

> weed wed when we med,
> said,
> we head weed head five millenia.
> cannabis canvas.

egyptian prego ain't let go she said gimme that hello there it is and it's a baby blunted halo.

play dough.
lego.
hungry hungry hippo.
hippo, hip op, hop op, hip hop anonymous. what's wrong with us?
can't help but feel sorta synonymous

> derogatory rat but that fact an
> **epidemic** you can't snitch.
> kitsch.

you can't
handle this.
    dismantle mash,

miss much

squared^2

no hut squat, hobo on a cut.
no colour in capital.
race chase chase race
only fictitious. idea of a schism
cuz the medium is written.
no he didn't.
swell.
who all swallow pills of the filler of the killer of the realer realm?

this is the fractal usurper

sorry if it hurt ya. hurry it can dirt ya. jury of precursors. scurry for that nurture. bottle up your formula. drink it like euphoria. sell it i'm not whorin ya. emails sent its warnin pa. pop one. pop two. pop three. stop. can't we all just get along? new kid on the block. swag. can't get a grip it write all on its own. black flag. red. white. no. anti-hero. non-zero sumness. just a little rap might get regular assumptions. nothin. being and existence, existential crisis is the rap of resistance. anthropomorphic. a kinetic alphabet would make you more sick. endorsin endorphins. raise the dead from their coffins. no voodoo linguist can compare to this gift. they just capitalist cults. i be protractin results. correlate more to date up to fate. amor fati. save rappin in latin for later cuz this here is more like me. never know what's in store so i liquidate my whole i.d. situate on plains not consistent with a-z. para. p.a.r.a defined as beyond. beside another way. linguistic. complex or simplistic? that's according to how you see the babel of babylon and who you listen to babble on from the rabble. left with rubble. spread across eons. use the bits and pieces like a puzzle never near completion, always out there reachin, breachin new terrain, said it once, say it twice, jump all over plains,

domains
like
academia
bulemia.
underground-philia.
rhizome at the root.
never grow up.
only show up
random.
non
linear-
quasi
cyclical
tandem.
¿transmit:inject:receive?

☙

hold him

reason's guards took gravity the storyteller to the stochastic holding cell high in reason's tower. there's only one way but down, storyteller. hahaha, all the guards laughed. meanwhile reason was in the war room preparing a counter-strike against the opposing forces. reason's fort palace was shaking, it seemed to come from the inside out. general, have you managed to locate the source of the disturbance? no, sir, well, sir, we fear, actually, that it may be coming from...*coming from where?!* from underground, sire. from underground? *what?! but how can you be sure?* we're not yet, your decadence of discipline, but we have reason to believe so, for there are only commoners outside the palace. the sounds of the beasts howling from the forests outside the kingdom walls were suddenly heard. *and what, general, is that?* the creatures, sire, from the forests, they seem to be reacting since the disturbance began to rupture. *has gravity started the narrative yet?!* no, my lord, it has not. *well then what are you doing! we need time! get gravity to tell! get it to start story telling again! by any means necessary! i need it alive, but not well, general, do you understand?* yes, your excellency. the general ordered his second-in-command to go the the tower and get the story out of gravity. listen to me second-in-command, you heard what our royal logic said, get that story! for the kingdom! for the kingdom, sir, yes, sir! god speed. second-in-command left the war room and was followed up the tower by his guards. now general, said reason, come here, i have a plan.

 up in the tower second-in-command arrived at the gate of the stochastic chamber. open the door. yes sir. the guards opened the door. gravity was there, stripped naked and suspended. with nothing to say there were no words, thus no story for it to have to orbit. alright gravity, do you know where you are? still nothing. this is the stochastic chamber, things will become very non-deterministic if you don't cooperate. we need you to start the narrative back up. still nothing. god damnit! you want to make it difficult for yourself eh? well i won't let you off that easily. rather than make it difficult for yourself we thought we'd have a go with your friend, electromagnetism. gravity looked up. i've got your attention now, don't i? ha. you wouldn't want me to hurt e.m would you? would that hurt you? it would, wouldn't it? good. now before i have to force feed a dictionary up your ass, you better start spitting out that story…that's it…good gravity.

☙

it was a bit before three AM, the party had died down, the workers went home early, so did most of the light weights. there was a group of seven on the roof, including edgar and rebecca. they'd both hit their maximum drunk about two hours ago, at that point they found a quiet corner down the hall from the loft to make out and flirt for a while. edgar had shared his plan for making money this summer. so i figure i can email every publishing company in north america, or even the world, and tell them i write reviews for magazines and newspapers. i'll ask them for review copies of their new releases. i'll have a few hundred books and just sell them all. boom! a one time deal heist.

now they were on the roof, the conversation had turned to bigotry and subordination. so this faggot called me a nigger, said max. it was more like thanks my nigga. but ain't no way in hell some punk ass pip squeak faggot gonna call me a nigga, *his* nigga on top of it. a girl named leeloo called max a bigot. well who the fuck is he to call me a nigger? who are you to call him a faggot? because he acts like one. i got nothin wrong with gay people, hell, some of those fuckers could beat the hell out of me...and make you their nigger. max looked at her and burned for a second. but he's all...effeminate? ye, anyway, i told him if he ever used that shit around me again i'll be sure as hell to drag his ass outside and make him cry like the little bitch that he is. you're a bigot! that's bigotry! call me a bigot, i don't give a fuck, if you don't wanna hear it then you can get up and leave. no, she's right, said rebecca. anyway, can we talk about something else? edgar mentioned that there was going to be that eclipse this week. nobody said anything. is there anymore booze left, asked the guy laying down, half passed out.

they were both pissed off. listen, i only called him that because he called me a nigger first, eye for an eye. don't justify yourself with that type of crusader shit. that just leaves everyone blind. well there you have it, said edgar, well argued. rebecca whispered in edgar's ear. okay. they both got up and climbed down the latter and went back inside. so many arguments today, i'm glad that one was resolved without much bullshit.

back in the tower

why have you stopped, yelled second-in-command. agent, administer the first tensor treatment to e.m so our storyteller can understand the 'gravity' of the situation. you don't know what you're doing, said gravity. pardon me, storyteller? there's only one story for you to be a part of right now. keep quiet or narrate for the kingdom's continuity, storyteller. think not what the kingdom can do for you, but what you can do for the kingdom! has the kingdom not brought you to where you are today?

if i look at where i am today i'd say the kingdom's fucked me over pretty good. yes, storyteller, your situation isn't all that favourable right now i agree. why did reason lock me up here!? what did i do? you are invaluable to our majesty in more ways than one. but enough of this, we're wasting time, we must make time. this is your last chance, storyteller.

you'll regret this, you son of a bitch! frankly, she was a bitch, concurred second-in-command, she reminds me of e.m. agent! the tensor treatment! you really are a fool! ahhhhh! don't think we haven't studied our tortures. i'm actually the one who designed these experiments. if you must know, everything is safe in our quarantined vec...(the entire tower shook, dust loosened and fell from the ceiling)...tor spaces?

oh yeah, and i bet i know where you keep that, underground maybe? how could you know? you're fucked now no.2. tell the narrative storyteller! if you care about e.m you'll tell the story. there's still enough vector storage space left to completely dismember her. so go on! tell! story tell! no.2 looked out of the window of the tower, nervously. the creatures and beasts of the surrounding forests were getting louder, sounding nearer, all the while the commoners carried on with their lives seemingly unaware.

☙

edgar didn't have much luck fucking rebecca. she wouldn't have anything of it. he tried in the quiet corner at the end of the hall, he tried to join her in the bathroom, he'd even tried before anyone had joined them on the rooftop. it wasn't going to happen today, not in any dignified and romantic or mutually lustful way. and besides, there was no more alcohol, she wasn't going to pass out drunk, not that he would do it like that, but not to say that the thought hadn't passed through his thoughts either. the boy knew his right from wrong in that regard.

none the less, with all his failed attempts at getting laid tonight, rebecca and him were still attached at the hip. a sign she actually liked him? they walked back into the loft. stevie, blais, prince, malachai, wanda and sarah were taking turns singing karaoke, reading off the projector. ah sweet, karaoke! stevie was just in the middle of singing genuine's 'my pony'. all seemed rather lively, not quite sober. wuddup guys, rebecca and edgar walked up. blais: is there a whole bunch of people on the roof? just a few people. bang bang bang! the neighbour slammed on the wall. i thought i heard bangin before, said stevie, through the mic. blais: okay, we gotta take it off. awww, stevie kept on through the mic. i wanted to sing some culture club. prince was upset. edgar stood over the coffee table and noticed two baggies. blais went over to the mixer and took the music off. he walked back over to edgar, that there is a bag of cocaine, and this here is ketamine. is that so? you wanna bump? sure. just the yayo. here you are my friend. cheers man. edgar took a bump off the end of a key. can i smell one more? if you want. and he scooped a key out of the baggie and sniffed into the other nostril.

rebecca? blais offered. oh, thank you. everyone spoke more politely to each other. she took a key. edgar: you guys have any more beer for sale? fresh out man. fuck. i'm sure there's a few half cans and forgotten beers lyin around. ye. edgar picked up a half smoked cigarette from the ashtray and lit it. wanda was still wavering back and forth, trying to keep her balance, she wanted to sing. When's it my turn? blais, why'd you take the music off, she said like a whiny brat. same time, different trip. cuz the neighbour's are pissed off.

bobby downtown

bobby had made his way back downtown. besides a fat lip, a bloody nose and a black eye he wasn't that bad. three good hits. although his gray tee shirt was stained. he'd used it to wipe the blood off his face. bobby sat down in the park at atwater to rest after his longer-than-usual walk from st. henri. he sat by the statue of john cabot aka giovanni caboto and rolled himself a cig.

   the park square was populated with a group of the homeless natives in one corner, some kids from the bars waiting for the night bus and a pair of the neighbourhood crackheads by the payphones calling their dealer.

    up rolled a regular face on his bike. bert was a disheveled looking motherfucker, thin hair, missing front teeth, but also dressed ready for work, steel toes, jean jacket, work pants. he;d often be seen walking around downtown playing the guitar and trying to make a little bit of money. he was a jack of all trades, a handyman, a good carpenter, but the truth was he was never able to kick that rock. one of the t.o.c.h.s, the original crackheads, from the 80's, that somehow has managed to not die from an overdose, be killed or thrown in jail. they just kept tickin. tockin. him and bobby were acquaintances.

    hey man, what happened to you, asked bert. some asshole was out to prove himself. shit man, sorry to hear that. hey, do you have an extra smoke? here, bobby gave him his cig. thanks. do you wanna buy some hash oils? naw man, i'm broke...how bout you fuck off! i'm not in the mood for your crackhead mooching bullshit, aright!? bobby got up, he was yellin at the top of his lungs, he'd become one of those drunks you hear yellin at people in public that give you the impressions that that's what goes down in that park. his arms were in the air, flailing, and heads were turning to see what the commotion was about.

    bert saw the cops driving slowly on the street that bobby had his back turned to. bert didn't say a word, he turned his bike around and peddled off from the direction he came. just keep biking, don't bother me again, how many times do i have to tell ya! then bobby found himself blinded by a light. what the? he turned around, the cops actually drove right into the park with their cruiser. bobby tried to turn around and walk away. you know the cops have nothin better to do when they bother with somethin like this. *arrête*! bobby kept walking away. *arrête!*

monsieur! bobby turned back around, huh, i don't speak french (that was a lie). what is going on here, asked the cop with a choppy but elongating québécois accent. nothing, i was just on my way home. where do you live? don't worry about that, just let me go home. the two cops were right in front of him, close enough to smell the alcohol. are you drunk, sir, asked the white cop. no. have you been drinking, asked the black cop. a little. did you get in a fight? no. then what 'appened to you, sir? i'm just going home. what is your address? may i see your hi.d? he reached to get his wallet that he never carried and: fuck you he gestured.

ah! the cops quickly turned him around and got him down on the floor. handcuffed. what is your name sir. mc. mc what? mc fuck you. You are under arrest, sir. his face was in the dirt and spit and cigarette butts. ahhh! what is your name? *ce con veut jouer?* you think this is a game? they picked him up and slammed him onto the hood of the car. what is your name, sir?! bobby delacroix, i'm from baton rouge, louisiana. i'm visiting my grandmother. i was mugged. they took my wallet. *américain?* how much have you had to drink tonight? i dunno? we're taking you with us, sir.

i'm one of you guys man. delacroix, its french. they didn't say anything and threw him into the back of the cruiser. bobby had a whole list of names he'd give the cops. bobby delacroix, bobby mcferrin, robert johnson, james delacroix, ahmad benanni, stephen el-mir, micheal selassie. mc fuck you, that was a new one. they never knew where he was from either, whether he said chicago, edmonton, baton rouge, jordan, yemen, belize, it didn't matter. he was never busted for anythin serious. yet. he spent the rest of the night locked up in the drunk tank and had an interesting talk about french colonialism, aristide and toussaint with the haïtian cop.

☙

he lay in the bare drunk tank. he couldn't sleep from the speedy coke he had earlier. he paced back and forth, sat down, got up, did push ups like he was going to be in there for the rest of his life. he still couldn't sleep. he lay in the middle of the floor and starting imitating mongolian throat singing. almost like he did reach some current that made him think about his life. and the downer crept up like spider's legs. growing up in toronto, his brother, his sister, his mother, his father was a rollin stone. if only mama woulda known, saw her stop herself from sayin she wish he'd never been born, all the stereotypes from that post-traumatic slavery syndrome. willie lynch said this'll fuck em up for hundreds of years.

then moving to montréal after high school. dropped out of university after his first year. there's always that pride pressure from his mother for continuing in post-secondary education, he never really understood it. what was he doing with is life? he had no idea what he'd be doing tomorrow. busking? would he get that job? he's all beat up. go to the okanagan? how bout tina? all the ideas seemed to go everywhere, non-sensically deriving from a past that was a life of its own. is this my life? is this me? my name? exist. live. love. death. like bert? preoccupy thoughts with the next fix, till i get it. i do what i want. no, what i can. what i want? i do what i want? what i want i do? i what? will? i do want? the can-can?

dawn

the sun was coming up and the last of the folks at the party were sittin by the canal. they were still laughin, some of them were out of their minds. wanda was crying in a k-hole, the acoustic guitar was being passed around. cigarettes. a joint. licking the freeze off the ripped open baggie. too drunk, stoned or too tired to fuck.

☙

a simile. a synonym adrenaline is tellin em. chuckles in the forest. running naked through the woods. bare feet on moss, wood and stone. the dandy hears my thud. breakin bricks cuz i could, can and will. what's this canon built? broken me cuz i'm mad and killed. bust i'm comin through. not for you, no reason, no purpose for your high arching circus. centralize, i de-.construction, i re-. production. proof and proceed.

౸

second-in-command rushed down the stairs. you excellency, general, i have a concern. you have nothing to be concerned with besides the storyteller to tell. but sir, they storyteller told me something of pertinent gravity. of course he would, yelled the general.

no, what is it, said reason. your excellency of majestic logical decadence sire, i have reason to believe the rupture is coming from underground, sire. is the underground secured? *why of course it is, but, oh my, the vector space.* yes, your sire sir, the vector space. the inner product is being quantified by e.m.'s tensor treatment. if the vector spaces are ruptured then e.m will be free. *but as long as we have gravity narrating everything should be fine?* no, sir, seemingly not. there is a chance, sire, that the rupture is incalculable and non-metric. if it succeeds to breach through from underground it will surely open our metrical inner product. your logical majesty, this could mean the end of everything as we know it.

goodness gracious me! how can we be sure that the rupture-disturbance is coming from underground? **the entire structure trembled** more violently than before. books from the library began to petrify and fall from their shelves, shattering. i fear the worse, your majesty, for its nature is incalculable. *what type of war machine is this!? why haven't i been informed about its possibility or probability earlier?! oh never mind, it is too late.* it seems to be coming from everywhere, sire sir. we cannot locate its precise coordinates shook second-in-command.

very well second-in-command, return to the tower and make sure gravity is stable. yes sire! general. *the time has come. release the surplus inventory. we'll profit from the vector space to draw the rupture right where we want it. then we will release the inner product on the surplus inventory and force the rupture to consume it all before it can breach. the inner product will be so concentrated and plentiful that it will send the rupture back to nothing more than the dark filth and shit from whence it was conceived.*

that's brilliant, your majestic reason. *we have no time to spare, general, act now. for the kingdom. for me, general.* logical reason kissed the general passionately. yes sire, for you! for the kingdom! he ran off to prepare for battle.

3
one week later: saturday: at work

cal finished his cigarette at the employee entrance of the king james hotel. he was fifteen minutes early. he had time to eat breakfast. he walked past some of the front desk people, some who had a pompous sort of attitude to them, like they were better than the people in the back of the house. he swiped his card and went into the cafeteria. they had free milk and cereal to eat every morning. rumours circulated that that may stop.

if the cafeteria chefs were able, meaning if they were ahead of schedule, in a good mood or not too hungover, they'd make eggs or french toast for breakfast, or at the least get some food from the fancy restaurants upstairs.

hey guys   cal's co-workers   scattered around the cafeteria
                    drinkin coffee with toast.
                       in front of one of the two t.vs

    @ either end of the room   reading the days newspaper or
                        sleeping on the couch

the south shore crew were all on time today, they commuted from the south shore of the island. whether they drove, took the bus or the metro, they'd be able to come up with legit reasons to be late. cal scooped some raisin bran into a bowl. he had the option of that or cornflakes. he chose the raisin bran because it kept him regular, which gave him a reason to leave about an hour into the shift so he could go take a shit. it was that kinda job, for a lot of the people working there anyway. if you could go **fuck the dog** for a while then go right ahead and fuck it. they were *unionized*, well paid, they could get away with anything.

cal sat down at the table with fred, kyle and jean-philip. they were a few years younger than cal. they were prone to getting into heavy conversations about science and technology that cal enjoyed discussing. good to be in that kind of well-informed company.

    wuddup boys? wuddup kale. pounds all around. cal didn't say anythin.

ya look a bit fucked. ya malin, not much sleep one day   schedule is off
       said kyle.   too much sleep the next   fuckin hell, cot damn schedule

balance.balance.balance.balance.balance.balance.balance.balance.balance.

                                                                          waste of time: *times of waste*
getting used to the full-time again i guess   full-time what:
                                                            can't partly waste time – fully
gotta make that **money** though, right? that bling dollar oh *high saviour* i respect and loathe
                   said jean   kinda   if i had to care

check out the car i'm going to buy.   smoke? the three of them concurred. fred pulled out his i phone and showed   cal, you comin? ya, i'll be there in a the picture. a 2006 mustang gt bitches.   minute. okay. twenty inch mags, lowered, chrome exhaust. i'll be able to smoke that turbo civic of yours.   they walked off. he's lookin rough today my 4.6 l's got 300 horse. mine'll beat yours they said. ya, really eh. off the line any day. twenty bucks says otherwise. fifty. deal. you're going down.   hey, did you hear about the new big foot fred, cal, you're witnesses. the bet's on. sure   research... thing.

cal picked up his bowl and slurped up the milk and raisins. charlie walked over and sat down with a coffee. ehhh calvin kale, you look like shit. ya been up bangin bitches all night or what? naw man, just tired is all is all ¿is all?

    charlie was an uppity guy, always in a good mood, a jokester. he decided to settle down, leave one lifestyle for another and got married and had a kid. he still talked about the good ol' days when he was cal's age. **yayo up the fuckin wahzoo** he'd say, not literally though, except for that one time. i'd get the broads to stash it in their panties, he'd say. you ever **need a job** just let me know, i know a guy. now he wanted to play it safe, his wife would kill him if she found out he was back into that shit. he had a good stable job, and even though the ***dirty money*** was good, there was always the chance of getting busted or killed and game over.

⁜

cal tried not to express his displeasure of work too much. he thought it always came out as pretentious **work to live** like he was above it all **live to work** like he could be doing so much more with his life **work to live**. but really, **work to live** what else could a high school degree and a couple of poems get you? it sure as hell wasn't **live to work** an impressive resume.

we got a full house today kale cal, lots of laundry to do! charlie laughed. yeah, i'm ready. four minutes left before he had to punch-in. gonna go have a smoke quick. (do my thing. chill vs. heat) see you on the inside. ya mahn.

cal brought his bowl by the dish pit. cedric the dishwasher: what's up man? another day another dollar man. ya brother. cedric drew the best hantai pictures cal had ever seen, not that he'd seen that many. cedric was able to draw you up anything you asked him in under five minutes. a real talent. *they say cedric only slept two hours a night and that he still lived with his parents because he was addicted to spending all his money on whores.*

cal realized there wasn't any time to smoke and had to go change into his all white uniform. he walked into the change room and gave the nod to a few of the guys from other departments. he opened his locker, no body was in his row. cal was trying to get used to changing in front of the gay latin guy whose locker was beside his. pedro was his name, but he didn't care what cal's name was, he just called him bello.

change into uniform. take a piss. swipe card. all the chambermaids and housemen would hang around and wait for their tasks and motivational speech from the supervising managers, who coincidentally were both the mothers of fred and kyle.

※

walk into laundry department. it was **intersection** going to be a hot and humid day. you could already tell because franklin, the big **highway** bellied bastard, was already sweating. cal had managed to become the weekend washer, **intersection** which meant he loaded and emptied the four washing machines with laundry. he was **expressway** also in charge of the massive dryer. he walked down to the end of the lengthy room **intersection** to where the machines were. he walked past magalie, the beautiful mocha skinned **information** haitian girl everyone stopped to talk to. she worked by herself doing the guests **intersection** dry cleaning. then there were the two towel folding machines. seemed like quiet **identification** and franklin were on those today. that was mr. quiet's real name, and ironically **super highway** enough he was quiet, but always attentive and watchful. a big smiley face **intersection** when he wasn't looking serious. he ended up losing his mind one day, he just stayed **intesection** quiet, the only reason why people knew something was wrong was because he stopped **intersection** sorting the king bedsheets from the queen sized bedsheets and just stood there, even **intersection** when it was time to go on break.

then there was thibeault, he had the **intersection** hardest quebecois accent in the hotel, maybe in all of downtown. according to him **intersection** everything was always diggydoo, whatever the hell that meant. he would be **intersection** at the receiving end of the bedsheet folding machine. but before cal could see who was **intersection** sending the sheets there was the laundry shoot. this is where all the dirty laundry got **fly** sent from all the twenty one floors, the one thousand and thirty six rooms, plus the **intersection** restaurants. this room wasn't for the faint of heart and was manned by the south shore **highway** gang. it was good for them because besides being the dirtiest and dustiest ob, it was one **intersection** of the more physically demanding jobs as well. you never knew what you'd find either. **expressway** some days some rich cunt would forget a wad of cash in his bathrobe pocket, it would **intersectional** come down the shoot, that's why you were best to always check the robe pockets. if there **way** was a prom party in the hotel you'd find cherry blood sheets, vomit. you'd find shit, literally, **way** some sick twisted fuck would pay three hundred and fifty bucks a night to end up shitting in **way** the middle of the bed. then there were they mouths, a lady who whose diamond earring **some way** were so heavy she feared drowning in her soup so she took them off and forget them in a **intersection** napkin that got thrown down the shoot. or the worst story of them all was the one about **way** discovering the dead baby wrapped in the sheets.

    at the end of the sheet fold and press **a dao** machine were amber and dominik. cal had a thing with amber in the past. she was a nice **way** green-eyed girl with a spray tan. it was rumoured she had some kind of unknown terminal **theory** disease. once, when she was lying in bed with cal she said out of no where, i'm dying. cal **intersection** couldn't believe his ears and when he asked her to repeat what she said she replied, i didn't **express** say anything. that was enough for cal to never have her over again.

    then there was the huge rolling press **express** machine used for pillowcases and napkins and other restaurant stuff. the machine's counter **way.ion** was broken and you had to count each article that passed through the machine in your head. **intersect** you can have my body but not my mind. at the receiving end was jimmy the greek. he came **high** to work dress in a suit and carrying a briefcase everyday. he was half senile, about sixty five years **way** old and spoke seven languages. the woman working with him was the uber-religious edith. she **like** was probly seventy or seventy five and had been working in the hotel since it opened in the **global** sixties, which is also when she immigrated to canada from barbados. cal had told her his **gentrification** grandma was barbadian and would always ask, how's grandma doin? you take good **by** care of her don't you and squeezed cal's cheek. she didn't believe jimmy was senile at all and **gentlemen** accused him of faking it. she wasn't the only one. and then there was laura, pronounced **of** louda, and iulia. they spoke in portuguese all day. for some reason cal couldn't shake the image of **gentle** iulia dressed up in a carnivale costume, bright green shimmering bikini to, shaking and dancing. **birth** he wasn't even attracted to her. vachon, the supervisor was putting on the switches to start **too pusillanimous** the machines. the huge stream rollers lowered by loud hydraulics. **and (true) pretentious**

you could never say much to vachon, if you had a problem or some comment he would often just go, yah yah, very positive but like he wasn't ever really processing what you'd say. that wasn't all the employees of the laundry, since the place was unionized the schedule was based off seniority. but for today, this was the weekend crew. it was summer, the hotel was busy and there was laundry to be done.

                                                        four machines to **start** them up.
                                  function keypads of all
             to the control
cal went
.   there wasn't any
                    laundry
                                to **put** in the machines yet so he
                                went to the shoot to help out

                    grabbing a notepad and pen, the ones that the
          to the other end of the department again,
    back
he walked

hotel **offered** to guests.
                he **realized** quite quickly
                         after being **hired** that
                         he'd **lose** his mind if he didn't
                      pre-occupy it with his own
                        thoughts.
                        ironic?

he **wrote**: when did back of the house **become** the back-back? was already **bubbling**,
his mind
 :how far back can i be **pushed** until i **fall** right out the back door?

he **entered** the shoot. alright. you fuckin slackers   the shoot was actually empty.
                                                              well, well, well…

fred was **sifting** through the restaurant linen half-assed, kyle **stood** with a broom in his hand, just in case someone **walked** in and he could look like he was **doin** somethin. jean-francois was blatantly **doin** nothin but **weighing** himself on the scale used to weigh the laundry.
   who was **workin** last night? must of been claude. he rarely **leaves** the shoot unfinished. hot damn. kyle **pulled** a hacky-sack out of his pocket and **started** up. not a second later edith **walked** in with a few dirty pillow cases. what ya be **doin** naw boi, da boss jus dun **showed** up. better **put** that away. kyle kinda **laughed** like a kid. okay. she was **looking** out for them.
   then there was a slight breeze in the windowless basement room. where's the barricade? shit, where is it? *here it comes!* the four guys **scrambled** around the room **looking** for the plank of wood to put at the end of the shoot's table. shit. the laundry **came** out that hole with all the dust and shit and **shot** all over the floor.
   god **damnit**. here it is. fred **found it**. good job boys, **snickered** cal **breakin** their balls. fred **pushed** what he **felt** like back on the table and the rest of the floor, then **placed** the plank so no more would **fall** out. it **doesn't** matter, the laundry'll **be** ten feet high by launch time anyway. it **became** a damp, dusty and mountainous play land if they **couldn't keep** up with the volume of laundry **coming** down. okay let's **do** this. they quickly **filled** up two trolleys, one of towels, the other with sheets. jean **brought** one trolley to the back, cal **took** the other. that was the routine for the day. thanks man. no problem. jean **returned** to the shoot. after a few hours he'd be even more **pleased to leave** the shoot and **bring** those trolleys back, unless there was a good song **playing** on the radio. cal **loaded** the two machines and then **realized** he **didn't** have a radio of his own back there.

God's Wife and the Synonymous X

he **snuck** out of the department and **walked** down to the very end of the corridor until he **got** to the houseman's storage room. everything the housemen **needed** to keep the hotel rooms **stocked** was there. the room was empty. cal **pocketed** some mouth wash, the good soap they **kept** for the gold floor clients, some of the good shampoo, then he **saw** the last radio **sitting** on a shelf all by itself. he **couldn't be seen** with it. he **looked** around for something to **put** it in. he **heard** someone **walk** in the room. he **froze** then **tried** to **act** casual and **grabbed** toothpaste and a toothbrush.

one of the housemen **turned** the corner. it was tabby, a short girl with glasses that really **liked** talking to cal. oh, hey cal! she **giggled** a bit frantically. hey tabby. what are you **doing** in here? just **getting** some toothpaste and a toothbrush. i **woke up** late and didn't get a chance to **brush** this morning. oh, well you **smell** fresh to me and **stepped** towards him, **smelled and laughed.** ha, ye, uhhhh, hey, **it's goin** to be a long day, can i **grab** that radio. oh, sorry cal, i just **got** a call for the radio. she was very serious about work. but if i **find** another one i'll **bring** it to you. oh. okay. thanks. ok, well i **gotta** get (before you're got) back then. cal **took** a step back. okay. later. bye cal. he **went** to the locker room and quickly **emptied** the contents of his pockets and **got** back to the machines before anyone **noticed** he **was** gone.

☙

there were now two more trolleys back there	to load into the machines.	he filled up the machines. he turned around and saw kelphasse talking with vachon over some papers.

normally, if cal:cal was waiting for the machines to finish finish washing ashing shing hing ing

cal was wait.*waiting for the* **machines** to finish

	he was supposed to go to the shoot.
washing	kelphasse hadn't noticed cal and cal watched as kelphasse went
into the	shoot (–go ahead,
shoot)...	

looks like he asked jean to
untangle ▶ the clean bed sheets so ▶
they could be ready for amber and dominik to work more seamlessly ▶

eliminate the seam ▶

wrinkle **free**, no **imperfections**, more **efficient**, *white-washed*, **cleaner**, stainless, can you hide that stain, what about that tear? ▶ that tear will be okay, **okay** for now, but not for later, for later there will be **new** linen, cleaner, whiter, better fabric, last longer. wash cycles, hot or cold, two, three, four. code▶one-five-one, one-five-two, one-five-three, one-five-four▶**enter. abort. cancel. resume.** count, record, wash. one pillow case, two pillow case, three pillowcase.

cycles and circles	the roller is too slow, **look,**	they get the good soap standards
gentle, heavy,	everything is too dry, burning	and nice bed sheets
colour, colourless white,	too fast, all damp. stretch it out,	not the common comforter
hot, cold,	you're stretching it too much. look	for *your* everyday standards
mild, tide,	its ripped, would you eat off that	for our everyday people
said, fed, feed,	sleep on this. standards	*(when are you not)*
on the line, iron, press,	king james standards	we treat like gold cuz
straight, their coming out	gold floor standards	**the gold standard**
wrinkled.	those **higher** standards	everyone deserves to be treated

<pre>
                                       like
                  can't reify   ¿gold?
_____the_____to_____
                 _symbol_____banks_____
                    like   •
                   action
                  bronson
</pre>

 deify the method like: how would you like to pay for that? cash ▶credit ▶__
            your life ▶with my life of gold ranks

but some pay more
for the nice soap that doesn't leave a film eg: _____
on your skin and if the commoners complain enough they can be treated like

they are gold and sent up to the gold floor but everyone knows they just complain a lot but hey, if that's all they have to do for gold then shit on me all you want you golden bastard. complain and shit. shit and complain – don't come playin if you're gonna complain –

but the **standard** *of* **service** is the client's always right so if they want to shit on you, let them, that's what i pay you for, and i pay you damn well you lazy union piece of shit. you don't deserve another penny from me, every two years we negotiate your contract, every two years you go outside and picket, and so so so, solidarité. then it's like a publicity stunt when i go to eat in the cafeteria with you, you see i'm not that different, only the other four out of five days my secretary orders my lunch and i smile and eat with a napkin and eat with the board of directors and the **CEO** and i met the saudi like prince that owns the entire franchise of one hundred and sixty three hotels around the world, but he came to this hotel, **my** hotel. give him the egyptian cotton sheets, let him wipe his ass with the face clothes, make sure he has lots and make sure the garbage is emptied more than regularly. he rents out half the floor for him and his entourage, they are royalty, they shit gold, black gold, you better respect it, respect the dollar because you don't shit black gold.

clears throat, how are you *sir*, **prince abudabi** sir. do people call you sir back home? oh, haha, pardon me sir, well i hope you feel at home, sir, prince. i enjoy acting american when i am here, please, call me raj. oh, yes, raj, we are in canada though, sir, raj, haha, pardon, montréal. ohhhh america, canada, you are like american backyard or little brother, yes. oh haha sir, haha. the prince pats him on the back

our bellboy, simon, will bring all your one hundred suitcases to your suite, sir, raj, sir. if there is anything we could do to make your stay more enjoyable, please don't hesitate to ask. i would ashtrays. **ashtrays**? yes, at least twenty. i hate reaching and getting up for something trivial like enjoying a fine cigarette. **i pay american producer to make special blend** for me. ha, yes sir, no problem. i smoke to enjoy, not for *reaching* and *moving*, you know? of course sir, i ¿understand? is that all?

please make sure my friends are well taken care of. they are on vacation and have been working very hard so that i can make money. of course sir.

please, call me raj. right, raj. welcome to the king james hotel sir, your hotel, haha. thank you he said gratified

❧

cal **emptied** a washing machine. he had to **reach** in and **pull** out what was four hundred pounds of dry laundry, now **weighing** at least double damp. he was **sweating** profusely. he **hauled** it all out into a spring bed trolley, **filled** the machine back up with dirty laundry and **brought** the clean sheets up to jean to **untangle**. he

went into the shoot where kyle and fred were quietly **working**. hey, went kyle, did you **hear** that there's some prince **staying** in the hotel? he owns the hotel, said fred. oh ya? prince of what? a saudi prince i heard. crazy, is he here to **check** up on his worker bees? **he's** here with a whole entourage. they **got** like half the gold floor. he's **got** a room just for his luggage. **ballin. wonder** if he **tips** good? rudy **said** he already **got** a hundie off him. just for **bringing** up his luggage. **supportin** the economy. **runnin** the economy. probly. **can** hardly **call** him a philanthropist. more a misanthropist if anythin. it's hot as a mutha today. ye. Cal just listened. cal **stepped** on the scale and **weighed** himself. i'm **gonna go lose** some weight. he **took** of his gloves and **stuffed** then in his back pocket as he **walked** out. he **walked** past the boss in his air conditioned office. he was **playing** video games. the screen was **turned** away but if he **was** too busy to **look** up **that's** what he **was doin**.

    he **entered** the locker room and **picked** up the globe and mail. he **sat** down in a stall and **flipped** through the pages quickly. **headlines** and *politics* like so much in the world is **happening** in

dakar resistance and indonesia chickens to vancouver roofs and **feel** good stories and war and **bombings** and a cure and a disease and everyone **knows** but **it's** always new. **what's** in the book section?

the book editor **doesn't** give a shit about poetry. could **make** the world a happier place. maybe the editor-in-chief **doesn't**? or his boss **doesn't**? or maybe **it's** the owner and stockholders? oh but surprise, surprise, mclusky, fuckin mclusky,

ah **go** on with him then. fiction: a
story about lebanon. a child's book.
about the child's book and the
brain: neurofeedback **training**:
isomorphic revolutions. events at
 the casa, concordia, yellow door.

cal took out his notepad and pen and read over what he wrote earlier: *when did back of the house become the back-back? how far back can i be pushed until i fall right out the back door?* he continued. *where's that eye of it?*
    well maybe that wouldn't be so bad. hell, cut right past the field and into the woods. live off the land, go west? build a boat? naw, too indiscreet. counterfeit myself an identity and use it all up. seems to be the only way. no way around it. using up identity after identity after identity. just like how massa done do it. only i can tell myself where i came from and what my mother tongue is. was and could be. shit, i'll be the real self-made man. like the diagram, them four elements. restore? maybe since ari they never understood it. but i did, my body, a black kabbalah.
    who says i be runnin from who i really am? massa? naw. maybe go south, waaaay down south. get back home to the home i never known. i never known it, so i just keep on roamin. everywhere my home then. citizen of the world. just gotta get out the house, past the field and never look back. the law try and bring me back i just say, nuh uh, you got the wrong name, i represent him but he is not here. wrong man. he was a slave, i'm a free moral agent. by law you can't own me, so that man died. do you know death? what of it? can you tell me what happen when a man die? well, he be free, this i know cause my name died long ago. but you ain't so and so, they'd ask, and i'd say no i know but thanks. then maybe they get all scurred and say. he say he dead, but he right there in front of our faces. death don't have to be evil cuz you don't know it. i'm happy. look. shit. i can imagine how casper felt. and they ask, you can go through walls and i say, no, but i can go through all, i just gotta know, that'll take me to there and then my body

will be new again, same body, new body, plea body, nobody, always gonna be a nobody at some point, but then you take off, i'll preoccupy down the line, de-body, re-body, all in the same body. i spend my time making a tongue. then i get a wife and she made her own tongue. so we gotta learn each other cuz there ain't no body. and we teach the children and so on and so on.

they call me three fifth cuz i'm three fifth crazy, just cuz i don't need their two cents cuz it's the other three that made me. one dimension, two dimension, three dimension four? well if i got the first three how you goin to tell me what's more? you see, we ain't all the same like your biologism claim, i do things different, why try to keep me in chains? my body ain't your body, your person ain't my person, why you teach me to respect it when you get off and forget it. so i know that's you, like a forgetful ol man, but this here is where i stand. so check it, we stand side by side like those cot damn hippies. that black hippie, bobby, that got caught by bobby, only gonna stop cryin when he climb that mountain zion. he made me realize, i wanna settle too, but that zion long gone, i can't see tryin. truth.

cal flushed the toilet. washed his hands. when he got back to the department everyone was gone. it was break time. he went outside for a smoke.

the sun was blazing. the boys couldn't even be fucked kickin the hacky-sack around. they were all leaned up against the wall keeping in the shade. out walked one of the girls from the front desk. she was new and shy. fine as hell, looking professional in her jacket and skirt. cot damn, have you seen her yet? she's been here for about a month. the things i'd do to her. you wouldn't even know where to start. ya i would. ok boys, it would help if you both started actin your age not you shoe size. she was talkin to a douche from the reception office, gelled hair, smooth voice, managerial.

cal took out a pad a jotted: **the name you know will not suffice.**

what are you always writing? ideas. are you writing about us? cal thought, i very well could be. yo, who's got ganj this time? i got. burn at lunch? ya mahn. word. word one sun▶breaks already over. can i check my emails on your phone?▶again?▶i'll pay you. just use it. cheers. they got up to get goin, cal walked▶zombie-like◀looking at the screen. find what you were looking for asked jean. no.

cal emptied and filled the machines. he was thinking of how to finish a verse of a song him and bobby had started writing together.
   my favourite things have, everything they need to be / it's a perfect day, come take a walk with me / rain or shine, i don't mind / when will i meet you? at a quarter to five, if you make it alive, by the statuuuue. oookay. let's just make sure that we get home/and don't get stranded just like last time.
   my favourite things have, have no ending / some people thing that you should, stop pretending / day or night, in my dreams, when will i meet you. like nickels and dimes, innocent time, from a hilltop vieeewww/ be nice to the park people / sorry citizen i got nothin at all.
   he jotted down: down and out, high but dry when will i meet you / i got a five, you got a ten / we could get a feeewww = that works. he seemed to have exhausted himself, or he was completely mechanic with the machines. he didn't say a word or think much until lunch.

narrative's babylon

the general, suited up, had ordered agents to occupy the town in civies, ready for anything. the agents had believed that the tremors happening in the palace could be due to the buildings age and antiquity, not by an invisible, unknown, all pervading panopticon of insurgence. the agents couldn't hear the howls and cries coming from the woods beyond the town walls. but there was indeed something happening out there.

sonic:// manifestations (were) we.avvving polyglot intensities ◀hot and white▶accelerating and then dwindling.indling.indling. being absorbed **by** the landscape,

                        by the trees,
                        deflecting   off the rocks
                                                          and boulders,
rustling,   cutting leafs   and foliage.
    tearing through the earth, protruding in quick **bursts** of dirt.

reason was raging inside his palace how as the intensities from the forests accelerated. *what is that **noise**!!! **aaahhh**!!!!* he covered his ears.	the surrounding guards and agents were unsure of to handle watching their oh logical majesty not being able to cope with this impending and unreasonably abductive force.

for this they **revered** him even more, for he was *the* **authority** of something they could never know. the sounds:
    were inducing irrational imbalanced thoughts in his psyche.

<u>   *help me!*   </u>

he rolled around on the floor in front of his throne. **mother *of god***, *help me*! the mother of god? did he mean mary? the guards were confused and tried to figure out how the mother of god could help their majesty whom they thought was god. where is his mother? who is his mother? they questioned and repeated. the only one who may know was the storyteller. he had been around the logical majesty longer than anyone else they could think of.

the general was in the second basement level, as far down as the palace was rooted. he was accompanied by two guards. the force of turbulence in the basement was calm as they crept around in the deepest recesses of the palace's corridors. they came to the end of a hall that had appeared to of not been finished during **the**

construction of the palace some two millenniums ago. it was a dirt wall. what the hell is this? no time. this way. follow me.

the three walked briskly. general, sir, may i ask you what exactly is happening, sir? what do you think is happening, soldier? i'm not sure, it all seems to be▶ **happening too fast** to make *sense* of▶.

if that's what the problem is, soldier, then i don't think the kingdom requires your service anymore. sir? pardon me sir? you heard me right. now listen to me, if you want to make it through this you're going to have to stand your ground. **nothing is happening too fast** ▶ *you fucking baby*. they arrived in front of the vector space room. keep guard here, whatever happens don't let anything past you. this room must remain **secured**. i'll send down guards to **replace** you in due time. yes sir, sir.

meanwhile back upstairs in the loading dock, the agents had returned with all the **surplus** (tasty) inventory that they could gather. televisions and computers and tablets and gizmos and **gigabytes** upon **gigabytes** of spatial_____ *this will be filled* temporality that would never be sufficient enough provisions for consumptive producers, unless of course the occasion should arise where a force so unfathomably familiar to their deepest *desires* came along and **swallowed** it whole. the palace was scrambling and convulsing with activity. it's harmonic functions were being analytically stressed.

oh we oh, we oohhhhhh, oh we oh, we ohhhhhhhh. chuckles. oh we oh, we ohhhhhh. chuckles. the agents unloaded the inventory into the elevators and lowered to the) basement.

---

when the general arrived back to the sir sire's court the guards had managed to sooth the emperor back into his thrown. your excellency of majestic logic sir sire, the inventory is being loaded and is descending to the basement, the guards are on guard, gravity is holding it down and there have been no disturbances detected on the spectro-metric graph.

    sire? sire? what's wrong? what happened to him, the general yelled at the guards. sir, the noise sir, he complains about a noise sir. he said he needed the mother of god. but we couldn't think of where she may be. you idiots...

    we thought that maybe the story teller would know. the story teller? oh you incompetent cunts! logical reason sat slouched, nerved wracked, sweat, loss of colour, barely conscious of what was happening around him.

agent! come here, no never mind, i'll do it myself. i have to do everything myself. the general ran back downstairs and saw third-in-command.

third-in-command, how is the placement of surplus inventory going? everything is going to plan sir. good. guards, move aside.

the general opened the security vault and removed a container of e.m's vector space. almost all the vector space containers were full, which meant

there must not be much left of e.m, which meant that they must have been having a difficult time with gravity

telling the story, which would explain why the soldier said everything was going by too fast to make sense of and the general was having to run

everywhere and the oh logical reason was fading quickly. i must get back to the emperor. seal the vault and keep it closed, even if i come back, don't open it! yes sir!

---

the general ran back upstairs and administered a tensor transfusion of e.m's vector space to re- calibrate the majestic dandy's metric equilibrium.

    there we go. are we feeling better sire? yes, that's it. take it, yes sire, take it all!

---

the reasonable dandy of elegant decadence jumped up out of his thrown in a triumphant return. *ah yes! i am rejuvenated! stronger than before! all i hear are the sequential integrations of melodies the nightingale's sing in the gardens where the cherubs frollick with the quiescent fluttering of my divine divinity. aren't i divine by design? more fragrant than the heavenly rose dove's doved rose? deep inhale. my senses* are nubile and pure once again! this is exquisite. i can see into your very soul, general, and how flattered i am to know. bless'd art me. the vigour of a thousand beauties courses through my veins. and what's this. i can sense more? i am moving the molecules of material with the whim of my will. i am levitating. i must be a god. the law is my nature and the nature is my device. i call upon the silkworms and they loom me the finest attire. i desire the most succulent of feasts and the most tender of calves sacrifices its very life just so it can be consumed by me. the highest celestial bodies serenade me with music of the spheres that only jesus of nazareth heard on his ascension through the pearly gates. hark! hark! oh how heavenly i hark! and you general, my servile believer, my john, peter and paul, equater of gospel you are. oh but i, i from pre-ordained to holistically ordained. i shine! i inspire! i am all aspiration could ever want to be! i can even relinquish aether that was once gaseous debris of yesterday gone. no need for apologies, it is but a sublime gift i shower you with. yes, have more my indentured concubines, let me shower you in the glory my wondrous body radiates. shower in my light! bathe in my awe! hark! hark! yes! hark! and for a moment time stood still while a perversion of an extreme one hundred twenty days of sodom ensued.

lunch

it was lunch time now. the first half of the shift was done. how the hell edith was able to work in that heat at her age was a mystery. they, the hotel, had offered her a retirement package that any other person in their right mind would accept, of course, nobody knew what mind edit was in because she refused the offer. she had no family of her own, she spent her life raising her younger brothers and sisters. if she retired she'd probly die. her body depended on those machines just as much as those machines needed her to send and receive. to stack and count. there were only a handful of employees in the entire hotel that had been there since day one.

Jesse Chase

so what'd we have on the menu today? spaghetti and meatballs, burgers and fries, fish, potatoes, veg. nothin special, no chinese food or nothin? fish, potatoes and veg please. thanks. jello for dessert, nice. tired of that cake. the nicest thing about the cafeteria was the free stuff, like the cereal and milk and whatever there was available from the pop fountain. the seating at lunch was pretty clicky. most of the employees all had lunch at the same time, at least the back of the house. the younger guys from the laundry sat together, the older ones were scattered in small groups. sometimes the ladies would mix with the ladies from housekeeping, the portuguese with the portuguese, who sat separate from the younger guys of the housemen and the older guys who wouldn't sit with the younger housemaids who sat with some of the housemen and the dishwashers who always wanted to sit with the girls. there were no female dishwashers. and some of the old creepy dishwashers just sat and talked amongst themselves. the people from the gym were better than everyone else but were cool enough to mix with the beautiful people from the front desk who for whatever reason got along with the people from the gold floor that knew the people from the reception office because the guests on the gold floor always need to be received. and all the managers sit together.

kyle inhaled his burger and fries. i'm gonna go roll that joint. i'll meet you guys outside? ya man. word. you're done? kyle picked up his tray and walked off. fred, jean-francois and cal finished their lunch shortly after and went outside. they knew the routine▶.

without saying a word to each other they walked past everyone else smoking and took a left then continued on for two blocks. they sure didn't look inconspicuous in their all white uniforms. at any rate, they sat and waited in the shade behind the wall of a building. nobody knew what happened inside that building and nobody cared. as long as there was never anybody around they could smoke joints to their faces every break. we only got fifteen minutes left. the guy can barely roll a joint, you should of done it yourself.

    we were in my car last night and i let him roll. half the joint ended up all over the fucking place. here he comes. kyle came running from across the street. what took you so long. i was getting mouth wash then i ran into my mom. mouthwash? Paranoid muthafucker. you would be too if your mom worked in the same place you did. maybe i wouldn't work in the same place my mom did. just smoke a cig after and you won't stink. did you bring the visine too? ya. ok. cool. alright. spark it▶.

    they puff, puff **passed it around in rotation**▶ fred coughed. did you put tobacco in this. ya. you said you were rolling a joint, not a spliff. it burns better. i don't smoke my joints with tobacco. well sorry, i guess you can't smoke this one then. too bad eh?

    it's just better that way. beggars can't be choosers man. this is a gift, and god **said** (so), i give you every seed bearing plant that is upon all the earth...they shall be yours for food. amen. amen. can i get a hallelujah? hallelujah! they were content and high, too high to fail.

storm's eye

✦   ✦   ✦

vessel inward. tincture picture. frix-un.hook.hock.hack.horka loogie. who? the boogie. man. child. from. femme. sun den. dock. trem-ble. texture. treb-le. db. velocity. rip. vio-lent. bio-bent. cryo-cunt. robot.no.rubato.notation. rubedo voca-tion. inc.lin.a.tion. post-diluvian cycle might go. menstruation://

chordal ritardando. eff.lu.v.i.um.continuum.vacuous.shoot back out. isomorphous feedback. loop. **cycle**. might go. oh. object. break and enter. b & e. to b & e or not to b & e. that is this object. strong force. weak force. weak force. strong force. moore has. it. paradoxed. witt's √ -1. boop boop dee dee dap dap boom bap. that. back. ▶ speed ▶ gravity ▶ speed ▶ light ▶ iso.is.so. same.how some segregate. do integrate? in it? multi(p.le) chan chan.nel speak.er.tweaker.set.up.down.all around. clash. slash. dis. mis. nomer. eel. shockoustic. torso. **cycle**. morsel. no. oh know. meta.mathesis.onto.poesis. meta. releases. re. lea.ses. po. po. mo. we. en.sem. e.s.p.ble. ppl. do.n't.po po.poo.me.

russolo.intonarumori. break. break. break. bomb. bomb. bomb. **cycle**. sixteen cycles/sec = sound. sixteen cycles/sec = noise   x sound.gain. momentum. frequency.projection.gest. ure. dimension. rhy.thm.give.n.rich.in.parti.ial.harm.on.y.ex. in.ex.plode!am.pli.poly.tude.par.t.ial.spat.i.al.y'all.special.lay. er.ing.ing.ing. struck.ture à la con.cept. when. acc'd.or not. seven. seven. seven. para.metrix. o'noise, noise, noise. ripping. gripping. slipping.t- ripping.contra.dicting.diction. friction. fric. tion. this. dis? lib. i . do. pass the sea in silence. it
requires silence   silence. no. silence. ad hominem. vivandi. modus. corpus. codus. hocus. pocus. super. calalala.i must warn: sworn.e-read.time via space via simile via silly me. curiously. these. ambiguities. juxtapoz and he is see.sick. just.suppose. itchin.del.e-use@enter.ic-enter.ic.enter.i.c.q.enter. i. **cycle**.we.en.sem.e.s.p.ble.ppl.

gen.when?dlin = heiro-greco-glyph.not even the tallest man-man can match this anima-talisman.

☙

you wanna be google able you wanna-be googlin-able constipator. labour ÷   synergistically. verbatim. vex? next:no:gun.sho.one. we meat again my nemesis. ekphrasis. gene.sis. neme.gene.is.i – machine of multiple mayakovsky skies? maya my's? not i's. oh you! negative or positive you kant come along for the whole day. way.tao.mau.mau.sun.tzu. i've landed but i can't get up. up . up. and cube away. shoo. get now. hasharat!

cyberspace and cyber taste.er.act.test.er.fact.est un bat.smoking circuiteries. smoking circus trees. there might be fees but exp. ect.ience will be neurologically fed back. just up.to you. you you. to cube. cube. cube. dub. dude. if you're just going to be a weiner and wiener you can decode your recode to recall the decal deco that's over-undoing my body from my bones and ghosts of butterflies in my stomach acid. but that's been done. get off the roof. spin.oza outta here. but it hurts. seasons of hell and seasons of bliss come and go like the cold bite of winter's kiss. when summer comes that claim i miss.seven fold hibernia, the trees fall: **timbre!** chuckles yelled **timbre!**

but dandy reason can't control his pleasin. what an appetite. for the love of the mathematical plight. word math.input:put out like a slut.went from turnin tricks to castratin dicks to you knockin like a eunuch happy with fake tits. that's all fine and dandy, turn your name to candy, suckin your own lollipop just to get your jollies off. now that's narcissist without mysticism unto ethic and bad politic. your cult is capitalist. economy of the misanthropist. cultural therapy. no wonder there's a distance, see how fucked up you were when you started this whole system.

and how fucked up you are when you claim this true existence. corrupt up. you say personally, like a person anally disturbed, wipe that smile off your face, in this case, don't shake my hand in return. i'm a biohazard, quarantined like a germ, contained within these pages, discombobulatin to learn. makin u-turns, vagrant pagan concerns, heretic of order, oddly, who's made of more water, your conscience is lighter. my body waves great. more adept to adapt. ya boat in the lake. look to connect to fate. buildin cities outta nothin while i got a network that's made outta wait:genealogical geodesic plains, holdin it together, webs of synaptic brains i call a transmitter, same that do receiving, cuz the body is electric, cybernetically perceiving. let's move beyond the hypothetical, traditional phase, outta phase, inner phase, dialectics of the sine. sinner wave. standard four hundred forty hz. tried 339? 338? 337? 336? keepin it level in integers. integral disfigures. out of tune pop singers. just poppin from the altitude. amplitude. negritude. abuse.ab.use of some bamboozled blaxploit gone wrong? might echo phoneticized ready-mades. negative or positive necro. skip. blitz. schizo.phono.elia. fanon. not far.off. decolonize or die. but. canaan.after schismogenesis. stabilize. can't. stab.ill.eyes.all. i's can't see. fancy. fant.s.y.can't we. just take that can't out from.cabulary. voc.ab. ad. image.in.aria. for all walks.a.hegio graph.ill.o.g.i.cal. doxa. this husserl. hustle of proto.geometry takes shape.**cycle**.there.territorializes and crashes on the rocks blue green pine tree. whale dasein blow hole mist. saleen twist. arrival in density.dispersal of amenities in quick moss from sun shade and loom wait. inhaled by lungs. digested through tongues. taste smelling tactility of how one hears their sight like kung's visceral fu. feng shui. done do wavering upward spotting smoke signal. chromosomal.chrono.soma.on backs of packs like rats in fur.in.fer.occ.ur.medi.ochre.smear.under. cadmium tears of red. passages products over time = bad = but: don't over compensate with monsanto – like trakl: of what you can't see cuz you can't look how you can't be cuz the company can't have it. bureaucratic stereo: the type that cause panic.that take you take for granted the nature of the planet.infected:by product.gimme trance.the spit of liquor shake and bake voodoo trance. beasts:shaman.priests.neitzsche leech.bullied geeks. on retreat are geeked bullies.distorted derelicts dare to wreck a trivium.damned and damaged delinquants absorbing academic idiom.miscreant poesis.fav.revolt than complacent peaces.cuz there never has been, but their better half: will: is the life in death.create in destroy.purpose:for the fun:some so serious.we toy.appearances.decoy.pass it off.just a cough.lead to fatality. boy. diseased.girl.pacify maladdiction.joycean cataclysm.radicalism isn't a million monkeys typin. a million ideas thinking.

so real similarity is pre-prepared these days?and frightful? an artificial intelligence of particular inference. for instance. fuck you. thank you. what is this? huh? is it the glacial ebb conglomerate of media holdin ya down and beatin ya? that's just the background. the high rise buildings fallin in, fish head, eye rotted out in the gutter, the stink clinging to your receptors, ol factory tapped, the mind reacts, how much time did that, or did it, that, that did, it was done, done did, you done did it, from end to beginnin, or phased half there and half past. fuck the hour, that's taxed ass, stick a flag pole up it and call it half mast. that passed gas excuse of a plan, i got no use for it man, you can't call me a fan, i would vote for either one of ya, you of the same clan. you. you. you. accusatory me. but there really is a problem. i live for liberty.

☙

if you're steady preachin for the dollar and the glory writin stories for a product of the product just don't bother with a fee.not so easily.rather teach grammar, keep it real, keep it measly, small commodity, not an idol like some vital organ of a body, that's a hobby, then we always oddly, it turns out that, a one celled organism can't get enough, calls you on your bluff, snuffed, wake up and smell the day that you did it for the game, not capital cocaine.rough.tough.said it simple and plain, don't belittle me like a fuckin amateur didactic, i auto-dictate around your method so pedantic.it's only rap you say, this is battle accolade.nomadic weapon that can threaten.take down.and move on progression. common cushy guise.like the boy who cried.wolf.until the day the wolf came.starving and insane.a real dog.you only had a little bark and couldn't run fast or far.never knew the real noise that could tear you flesh apart:kill joy circuits bombin:rad. io.flash.starfish.prime.ya dun know the reprocushun cuz ya only be makin calculayshuns.step out in da field.the fallout and a.geomagnetic storm a brewin.dat's some clout.pumpin flux into syntax compression.bust.can't hold it in.hold it back.only gonna blow up.gamma ray knock.electrons.out of orbit.but electric gotta go.somewhere.it come a forcin.knock you to the floor.melt your body open. oscillating currents.need forensic approachin. frenzy commotion.alchemy potion.inelastic.photon. quantized. corrodin.mementum is rollin.the energy is foldin.so transparent you can't focus.that's why this topography.this abecedarium. aidin like a guide, waitin for you to see. usually beauty come in familiar form, until it's defamiliarized and beauty be reborn. you see it change in the style from century to century.based off the preference men mention.the one who love to hate his mama. metaphor for trauma.generations for generations. it's the general drama.shed the light on dark.the dark is colour spectrum.pretty basic shit, no need to keep guessin.get close to a theramin.the sound become very thin.till it like a pin-drop on the backdrop and it suck ya through a black hole.where ya gwan?ya dun know!bodily nnemp. the war machine ain't all seein.ya gotta be hooked up.off the grid?no data trace?idiopathic race?check the volts, check the watts, check the joules and you're fooled when a change in the system won't provoke an opposition this ain't anechoic.chamber.no diffusion.don't diffuse outer anger.outta reverb off of rebith.out of a coma.i heard a voice echo ancient crypt scripts by accident? it was bound to happen with all this white noise...

dispute

it was an accident. sorry. ohhh no now.
vachon rushed over.
edith was freakin out on jimmy.
    shit was about to hit the fan

her voice pitched ▶so ▶ you could hear it **over** ▶ the incessant droning and hissing, popping, folding, spinning, dripping of the machines. if you were far enough away ▶ you couldn't quite make out the words, you would just recognize the cawing tone of her voice, shrill.

jimmy backed up. he replied. i don't do anything intentionally
        in his nasally   he was talented
        foreign twist.

all he had done was knocked
over two stacks of pillowcases, the big, the small, they
                knock   now, about three hundred
of them. the fact they'd fallen on the floor made most of them **contaminated**. edith wouldn't let that slide, anyone else would usually pick them back up, shake them off, and pile em up with the rest of them. even kelphasse would, he wasn't quantity over quality.

i dun wanna work wit im! he canny keep up wit de **productshun**! he dun keep count either! vachon was trying to calm her down.

he looked at jimmy   who just stared blank and semi slack jawed. he was playing with his dentures.   he dun care! he **fakin** it! look at im!
                      i don't *do* anythink intentionally vachon.

it was ridiculous that vachon had
to mediate between two people old
enough to be his parents.   the man **fakin** bein *dumb*! dat only
make him *dumber*!

vachon had to at least make it
appear he was trying to help the
situation as   edith went off, berating in patois, she looked like E.T with glasses. in the   hotel robe she wore to keep off the chills
                      from the fan.

is it true jimmy, that you don't
count the pillow cases?   i don't count the pillow cases vachon.

for the past two months the counter had been broken on the machine, which meant you had to count every single item that came out of the machine. only the most pious employee would count everything with protestant work ethic. nobody in their right mind would let the act of counting articles of laundry occupy their mind for eight hours a day. it would drive you to the madhouse.

then kelphasse **walked** *into* the situation ▶   ello edite. what seems to be the problem ear?

        the funny thing was, as good of an employee edith was, she disliked kelphasse just as much as anyone else did. she started blasting him.

pardon? she wouldn't let him speak.   where were you when we need ya!?
    she set the tune like a   the man knock over all de pillowcase,
    grandmother would.   he dun count em either. i dun wan work wit im.

    **by now laura and iulia had stopped sending
    pillow cases and were around to see what
    all the commotion was about. amber and
    dominik had almost stopped sendin sheets
      too, so thibeault came around to see why.
      everyone knew how boring the job was.
        a little bit of action would break the rhythm.**

okay. evoree boughdee, back to work.
the 'otel is full, we ave a lot of work to do.
        everyone moseyed back to work.   dun touch me!
        kelphasse put his consoling hand   you not my
            on her shoulder.   friend! i

been workin here forty nine years! i never see this place run so bad! everytin be fallin apart. no wonder no body count for ya! tings ain't what dey used to be! you just happy in your air conditioned office. ya laughin at me!? ya tink i'm a fool! i raise me brothers and sisters! ain't no future here, that's what i tell the young ones. but i work to keep dis hotel runnin! where were ya when we needed you! on dat computer lookin busy? everyone say you be playin games! you tink you better than me!? i work hard boi! don't you touch me! don't you lay dem greazy fingers on me! everyone just stood there and listened. kelphasse took it all. it was epic. one of edith's best. i tell the big boss how you work. he listen to me! you'll see, you'll know! kelphasse was found dumb and dumbfounded. you'll hear about it, then you'll know! and if that ain't enough i'll make sure you get it! was the little old lady threatening him?

vachon was the only one who was capable of getting her to stop. edith he pleaded. edith. kelphasse couldn't do anything. besides, edith had the union behind her. it was time for last break anyway. an hour and a half to go. the machines all stopped and everyone left. kelphasse noticed the machines weren't running. where was cal? he went back to his office and played starcraft.

☙

the agents and guards of reason hut-hut-hutted along, guarding, builiding formations, preparing for what they could never rhemeta-torically prepare for. still, they moved, absurd contradictions and abstract tautologies, decadently defenseless. there were two guards who arrived in front of the vault in order to replace the other's shift. agents, they announced. agents they replied. and the two former agents left as they were relieved by the latter. the two new agent guards guarded the vault in conjunctive statures. there were no other agents guarding or patrolling the immediate vicinity.

idempotent, muttered guard number one quietly enough so that his voice didn't reverberate off the cavernous stone walls of the basement corridors. guard number two looked at him, eyebrows contorted in question. idempotent, said the guard again. what? idempotent. idempotent? what's idempotent? the guards face snapped and stared eye to eye. i.dem.potent. what is is. guard number two couldn't make sense of the situation. i.dem.potent what ises you fightin for. i dem potent what ises ya dun know. i dem potent what ises. idem potent noise. guard number two gasped....it was too late. he was consequentially reduced to phonemes. pop! and they scattered along the floor, syllabic redundancies that guard number one collected into a pouch. he chuckled.

    what are you doing, demanded a new guard when he turned the corner and saw chuckles rummaging on the floor with a mysterious pouch. what? he chuckled. what are you doing? idempotent. what? chuckles chuckled. idempotent.i.dem.potent. potency.i.dem.potent what ises.i dem noises://idempotency. ot.an.see.ought and be.and simile.the ground began to tremble. the new agent-guard's weapon wouldn't gerun. chuckles knew that if he stayed in close enough proximity to the vector space vault, he would be able to continue manipulating the existing tensor radiation being emitted from the sloppy containment of e.m.

    i.dem.like them.as.same.po.ten.tial.tial.tial.tial and the guard popped into phonemes all over the floor. the space was clear. the entire balance of the structure shook violently and almost knocked chuckles off his feet. this ability of dismembering the syntagmatic anatomy of guards and agents was enough to make chuckles power-drunk he had turned, he howled a noise, a rich and heavy cluster fuck that was heard all throughout the palace and out into the surrounding town. chaos ensued amongst the citizens. looting and pillaging that sound alone resonated so deeply into their psyches they lost control of their selves because they were never given the the to withstand the likes of it! the royal reason was just dabbing his lips with a napkin after a divine feast when suddenly shit hit the fan.

nearing the end of the shift

everyone came back from break. still no cal. kelphasse asked
around. had anybody seen cal? Had
    anybody seen cal? of course some of the guys had seen him
    asleep on a bench in the change

        room, but they wouldn't say anything. kelphasse went
    out looking for cal. as he went
        out one way cal synchronously came through the
        other way and went back to
            working the machines. emptying,

      cycle▶   turn, spin, fill, haul, the smell of laundry,

                the future▶   teach?
            everyone teaches. obstacles▶ what did
                he have to

lose

                    nothing
  move   around   apartments.   don't harm the

        people.   live   on the
    streets,   live   in

                the
              missions.
        move south,   it would
            be warm

        in   the
    winter time.   anything.

    miss family.   miss   friends.
would it matter?   starve?   steal?
    tough times.   no tougher   than

God's Wife and the Synonymous X

                    the third world.

what about the privilege.   for all that it mattered.
for time. that's why   he could lose. shameless. loss.

eternal loss to eternal gain.   repetitive dichotomy.

                                but the times,

                        oh
                                the times.

                                        creeping up

                                                        on him,

                                                                pins

                        and needles,
                        inflicting

                    acu-
puncture in all the wrong ways.   outside of time
all would stop racing.   that's it, deprive the senses
of time and time will leave me   alone. the objects
would stop spinning,   the words would stop spinning, temporality
would cease to define   spatial
mobility. go crazy   with time? discourseless possessions.

i saw **my** face in ▶
the mirror on the clock
and it kept turning and   winding   and   i pressed

                    the buttons for the alarm clock to
wake me up ▶and i need to check my email, my messages

▶bring this laundry. hey man, can i use your phone? **it's about to die**. sheet. okay.

    sheet. sheet. white sheet. stained sheet. okay, okay.

        ¿where were you?
                i was, i'm not feeling well.
      you are washer,
      you wash, on time.

i'm having problems.   **¿like?**
fuck, i dunno, insomnia, you

cunt. you wouldn't

congratulate me unless i force
fed you. gregorian anxiety
said to be strong like hermes.
unix calender me. but the
suspense of being   -suspended-   indefinitely,
the free-fall of impending
death, only insured once i land.
gravity pulls at all options.
angles. stretching the psyche.
in leisure? no.freeloading saints
allowed. cut a mulatto mullet
afro trash son of a becky.

be free from?   *for?*   esteem to it.   it,
how many times does the   vague thing   perceive   perceptive perps

   merked like   jerks?
                    it,   don't laugh
          you fucking sigh,   you might kill me
                jog on.   stop it,
                                  you're killing me

God's Wife and the Synonymous X

you're mad aren't you
angry at your daddy,
but really you're fucked
cuz you **killed your mom** and

raped your dad you twisted fuck.

       you wait for the moon ▶ to cross   so it's dark
                                                                                                    enough to
                                                                                                    avoid

the shadows,   shadows
                                                                                                   of words
                                                                                                   of shadows

you feel real fuckin cool   the blood is blue   you're real fuckin cool

                          that definitive elegance of objects,
                          this is an object, you sigh, sigh,

           dexterous   +   omniscient and ignorant.
                 passive relations.

arrogance absolved.
                       spite and spit and sun all keep
                                  dripping off
                                            dog-earred
                                                                    notes.
the page corrodes *by* the ▶ sight of it.   the words
                                                                                    linger on the

floor.

---

                                                                                                   stepped on.
                                                                                                   scrapped

                              and molded
                         but continue
                            on
              persisting.

if only   for a moment. passing
sentiments.   vice allotted.
it's all   behind. now.
swipe.   swipe. swiping ▶ faster.
the window is open.   constant exhale, huffing
in   perpetual motion.

                    there are no objects.
                         the freedom.
_____matter
_____became lazy.

                    cal, where were you?

reasons and excuses: i was sleeping, i'm sick, i can't focus, there's something wrong but you'd tell me some lame anecdote about your internship to get on the good foot. fuckin good feet.

                         get back to work!
                    i've got to beat the terrans.
                use psionics so i don't have to at home,
          that's when my girlfriend gets pissed off and i don't get laid
       and she jerks off beside me and looks at me with that look in her eye like
        too bad i have to do this cause you're just too busy for me, i'm jealous of
         your computer and the games you play with all your attention saved in
              that economy. she's an economy her self. i'm almost
                    going to *write* <u>you</u> **up**.

fuck, do you know what it is? poor mr.baxter. i killed him. he was almost already dead but i killed him. i'm not like that. i don't kill people. you killed someone? well...

need to get that money from bobby.
don't know why i let him money.
what the fuck was i thinking?
he said he'd pay me back.   and the student loans can go fuck
               themselves. the government wants their
               money they say. cot damn banks stealing
               my tuition. i wonder if this is it? losing it?

what time is it?
time allotted.
slotted.

psychological scene analysis.
composite regular.

the cycles are almost done. won't have to fill em up again. almost done. let me sit down. take my shoes off. here comes vachon.

suited up

reason is ready in his battle armour. the problem, said the general, is rising. running rabid. the vault is sealed but we can't get downstairs. well, we can but there's a raving maniac down there, it's not looking good, your majestic honour sir.

<u>*reason speaks axiomatics:one labyrinth after another: they will never succeed general. do you understand?!*</u>
i is another moore's paradox multiplied by a zeno-meta-phyiend, neophyte meta-theme. not so saturated, ubiquitous opacity, try to see the mindscape. climbing time scapes. momentous. paralysis.
   never met.a.move like an arrow.why does.del.use that flight?

i.dem.potent.claw, jaws, jowl hannibal, lycanthrope-like a lycopolitan wanna-be fool is uncontainable under the tide.

running, guards-a-running, agents-a-blooding-forget me phonemes. complex numbers. self-similar patterns thrusting and shattering and reflecting off the eyes of every victim. mandelbrut set rorshach tests disappear in and out of the shadows. the poetic surfaces that beat the organs out of bodies. gutts on the floor. adrenaline terror. homunculus phonemes scattered all about. they penetrated the pores of the guards and agents they would find and pop! the guards turned too. idempotent. idempotent. changed the little homunculus people. multiplying and multiplying as the wanna-be lycanthrope power-mad fool drooled and howled and was savage.

forget about the linguistic philosopher's stone. the magnum opus continued to spread without epic colonial time-bombs. a multiverse substance latching onto any skin it can. past. fractal souls caught in geodesic crystals containing colour. tesseract. glomes of thoughts bubbled out of the charts. the howls from the forests began to crack the earth. hell was freezing over and satan tried to escape, accusing job of being selfish. noah could be seen in the distance on a tidal wave of wine. he prophesied a land of heathens and pointed to nimrod for justice. isaiah said in your heart i will ascend, i'll be down, part of the assembly, on that mountaintop so sweet, but i'm low, so low. you dug my grave? or did i? i just wanted to be high! hiya hiya hiya me. hire me? hire me? hiya hiya hiya take me hiya, but you don't wanna hire me. transgress the law, the difference outside the system. self-perpetuating, self-justifying hypocrites. the signs that i bear aren't crimes. why would god create satan? satan is innocent, plead ignorance. but that would be a dialectic impossibility. this is unholy. who planted the knowledge tree and who planted the living tree? all i know is that the rhetoric won't allow me to. who in the devil is raphael? divine priorities, exegesis of labour, augustine? speak up! the devil wasn't wrong in calling upon canaan. now look, the dreaded fist of the north, the south, the east and the west. everywhere! and the hamites sent on without a care or second thought. and the pharisees, with bloody ink in their pots, scribbled away. all part of augustine's just war: no questions, no answers, you're just a killer. ask a question, but god won't let you. don't say anything else, it's just nonsense. but but but but nothin! just look around, you're surrounded by death, aren't you? some life. enough to make you crazy, or is sanity your deluded justification, that clear voice of a certain kind of reason. wail the axe. go on. righteous prick. can't you see the children cryin, brother's dyin, mothers whyin, that's why you shut her up. you fuck. was asherah in the top of the tower? locked up with e.m? was asherah your first experiment? where's the plot in us?

done work

okay. done work. that wasn't so bad. go to the internet spot? then see guys later. bright and early. ye.
    this is caving in? caving out? whose shadows are on the wall? folding from all sides. make origami out of the street. that building. it's a construct. ya ya....but it wants you to go inside, through those doors ▼ with the money in your pocket, if you had any, and buy buy hurry up ▶ and buy boi. the pretty sales girl will tell you what she thinks you'd look good in ▶ then we go out for dinner under a ▶ chandelier and champagne ▶ diamonds ▶ a ring or a necklace ▶ kids ▶a house and retirement ▶ everything will be alright.

¡crooklyn in the
house tonight!

saturday afternoon, everyone is out and hats and hair and sunglasses and sandals and kicks and shorts and skirts and pants and shirts and tees and tank tops and dancing elvis statue. you scare children. out of my way you walk to slow, hello, mellow, measure the chi and regulate. store. more. whore. which one?

rich one. poor one or lung of the red light. ding a ling a ling = a cold steel guitar and c.c.c.r.r.r.a.a.a.a.c.c.c.k.k. the bucket drum. people on their cell phones, cell phones cell phones. always on their cell phones, talk all day. gotta text a so and so, can talk to you bout hubris codes, you'd be sold in a usb key, unlock: leaked a wiki. mocked the g.v.t. it's not a free t.v. i got tele-vision. vision telepathic.if these ballers balled who'd be first round draft pick elite.elitist shit-squeezer.pip squeeker.ebineezer scrooge.go get ghost checked and ruined.make a room, put up posters, pictures and a mirror on the walls and what else do you need.

and the **clowns** are out now too. who let out the **clowns**? sinister **clowns** running around, weaving around everyone. pick pocketing. running across the streets, stopping traffic, dancing on cars, but nobody seems to mind. **clowns.** face painted ghouls. climbing through your bedroom window at night like slithering **clowns**. mother fucking type **clowns**. judgment day **clowns**. sealing fate **clowns**. forever like this **clowns**.

the friction of breathing heating against the pressures built up in the upper back, pushing down on trapezoid muscles. breathing and friction and mechanical breathing and friction, biotic senses being membranes of a dialogue. expanding and contorting tzim tzum. withdrawing in breath, tikkun here and there but it's pressing with more and more gravity. demanding attention. making life more disagreeable without it. so you agree. the shards of shevirat hakelim have splintered into my body, my eyes, my ears, my mouth, my nose, my neck, my heart, my back, my lungs and abdomen, my dick, my ass, my legs, my feet. i stand reflected upon. no transcendence. immanent evaluation brought to it's limit. but an idol. sadder than yahweh. nameless without him, only a spark on a spark, the same dia/synch-omatic womb we've been growing within, pressing against for millenia. wah wah. you can't get out so you can't get big. on an axis, with coordinated nets, turning pockets in and out, i am the pocket lint on tumble dry through this cycle. the great stories of the days makes everyone wanna be someone but it turned out that from the underground things didn't work like that because those great stories had to be dialectically removed from the image of the body's self. then a priori dripped. ipped. through the pages, from the ink and drip.ipping into the air, evaporated particles inhaled all the breathing and friction heat was pressing on, indian ink stick and poke tattooed memories in the karma tissue that is flesh absorption. absorbing the billboards to logos and songs that play everywhere, the ones you don't wanna hear and the styles and lines and fashions and trends and catch-phrases like what's the science, yo? literally. and the attitudes of the public, eating away. but to never taste it, when just looking fills the appetite because your system can only tolerate so much bullshit.

༄

storefront, bloody, storefront, storefront, fronting as a store, posing as an *idol*, an oracle, able to resolve what **ails** the common first world problematic. i feel sad, i will buy. i feel happy now. let me treat you. come **try** this out. what ails you. nothin, cuz i'm ill. shit. transform one slice of time into an opus, one word into an encyclopedia. what's your source? who are you? this could be your facebook. where does this all come from? a hermeneutic of the self like cocking back the hammer before the trigger is pulled. ready to fire off at any moment. dangerous or savin us? ready to live? it ain't show and tell. this is a regular tale. gonna fly. lumpen welfare principles with a nomenclature to match. spirit exercises. if you have to fill the vessel till it breaks and enters, tunneling ciphered siphons from the reserve becomes a swift tidal wave that would rush down to montréal up from the seaway valley. coming right down st.catherine st. from st.anne de bellevue to anjou, laval, greenfield park, maybe all the way to sherbrooke. the people tumbling down the streets being thrown and tossed by the current like a shark with a rag doll. just make it through the doors of the twenty four hour internet spot before the street is an ocean, before you had to do your groceries in scuba gear.

can i get thirty minutes of time. two dolla. computa thirty three. thanks. internet in me.log.in/data.time.date.ping ping.static snow.synapse.mind.looking for downloaded gratification.pop up unblocked.@ rate of amen.a response.uh huh, uh huh. what. well. it's personalized. it seems encouraging. but no reason. no feedback. you don't want it. that's it? is it not good? stye? what? ah yes, in the silence.

> the future, that closing in of time. i've been wound up around your spindle and it winds me tighter until the day the spindle takes no more to offer. the thread snaps and i have nowhere to go. but this is why i knowed not where it was i was going. the classicists call this obsession, it must be nice knowing where you're going when the gods are at your back and you listen to the tracks of two thousand year old scripts. do you really believe these pillars are eternal? that the earth is still flat? that yesterday will always direct today and tomorrow? listen to me, the past, and i will interstice your matrix so that you can achieve anything as long as you praise me and feed my children's pupils and their offspring.

| huh, maggie wants to add me? | her pics. she's quite fine. uh huh. | she's kissin a boy? though | from two years ago accept. |

| i doubt she'd cheat on someone with me. | spring break in mexico summer in morocco smilin. jokin. never can tell. |

:news feed:
:they schools:
:the intellectual hip hop resistance:
:the stimulator:

:she's always callin out haters:
:the scottish dialect is dope:
:he's back from the dentist:
:graffiti café:
:added a photo:
:shared video from demonstration:
:baobob:
:a poet making poem's techné from profiles of dada light:
:that night:
:need extras for a video:
:if deliverance is culturally significant:
:dr.pill likes:
:words for teenagers:
you adults, world runners and the elderly: good lazy chair: a review://
suddenly a loud yell!

the geeks were yelling   fuckin hell. cal gets up and walks   over to ▶ the counter.
and screaming at their   do you have any **headphones**?   no   mo
headphone.

computers, play some   **okay.**
game, *killing* some
body, reading **profane**   cal went and logged **out** and **left** the place.
eulogies **in scripts**.   he needed quiet. absolute quiet.

he need to hear john **nash**'s mission may be one level too far but there's
something that   himself how needed to be done.
jean baptiste   grenouille the vacation should be allotted in a one two
three week **interval** depending   needed to   on **seniority**. a theatre of
cruelty: **violence** and madness, the weak   **smell** himself.
humiliated, the cruel and cool, the maniac and the murder, despot and
genocide. silence will alleviate. being thrown into the mosh is
usually a go.

---

just chill out fuck. lemme call bobby. cal spotted a payphone across the street. and all the shit that happened in between is the **unsung** history of a **minority**. a reiterated **utterance** of speech-**acts** clamouring **for** roots. if only floating orbs of pale dream light were self-contained. that's not possible, maybe mediation would bring us closer?

☙

grandma is **knitting** quilt with the crown of 3 ecliptic birthdays she handed down to the next 2 generations sub one astral eclipse for calvin. the can man is at work. kids throw a can at him and laugh, here's a can for you can man. i **clinamen, no** can man, **clinamen. fuck you, thank you**, hahaha, he responded, the kids were just weirded out. they figured him mad. he was **mad(e)**. isabelle was **painting** in her living room. stevie was just getting to bartend for the night **shift**. dealer was in his apartment reading the copy of neitzsche that bobby dropped. his infant son started crying in the other room.

in the tower

listen, gravity, this doesn't sound. you haven't realized that without e.m. you can't make sense of this? like lack of oxygen to your brain, you begin to feel light-headed. that's enough! the time is now second-in-command. the world of abstractions is at its vivisection, reifications of the forest are already here. your words! these aren't the words i want to hear! do they make you question your reason? the reason? stop it! the other agents in the room jumped, they couldn't hear gravity talking in the mind of second-in-command. the alien vocabulary had its spell bound hypnotism and other isms punching its way out of the box which was his consciousness.

  the tower was high in the clouds. on the ground level were guards, ready but not sure what for. underground, in the basement of the palace, chuckles was having a ball. the general couldn't think of any other solutions. chuckles the dribbling madman had deduced all the signs of logic in the area. all that was left in the cavernous cellar corridors of the palace was the idle surplus inventory. it sat ideologically in place. waiting to be consumed.

    chuckles roamed the corridors collecting the last of the homunculus phonemes into his pouch. then, with ceremonious measure, he propped the bag against the wall and bent down onto both knees. he began chanting:a kala kumbaya shalom a lekum ichi ichi yo she:kon. konbanwa, si si dit le o.g. falasha habibi pun de four d hor-eyes-on. wht? wht? three four.

    the general was rushing downstairs looking to face off. a kala kumbaya, he repeated the chant over and over with more voracity, louder and louder and punched both his fists into the wall, penetrating and shaking the entire palace. *now what?!* wailed the dandy in his court. chuckles opened the bag. the little homunculus people climbed out and up onto chuckles' body.

he chanted kala kumbaya shalom a lekum ichi ichi yo she:kon and as the little people gripped and climbed all over this body and ragged clothing, he punched his fists deeper into the wall, his arms in up to his elbows, he let go a final **wht**? **wht**? and the homunculus all ran along his arms and burrowed themselves into the earth of the walls.

    the general was creeping around the corner, having troubles believing what he was seeing. when the sight of the homunculus one by one jumping off chuckles' head, shoulders, arms and knees, had lost its novelty the general turned the corner ready to destroy chuckles.

    fool! what are you doing over there? chuckles opened his eyes and turned to see who was there. the general raised his pistol and fired from about fifty yards away. he hit chuckles in the chest. chuckles lay on the ground whimpering like a wounded and dying dog.

    so this is the savage that was causing so much trouble. how many of my men did you manage to kill? you son of a bitch. son of asherah, chuckles replied. what? chuckles started spitting up blood, he was trying to limp and scuffle back on the dusty floor. asherah? the fairy tale that gravity told of? only a fool can fool himself, there are no sons of asherah because there never was an asherah! the general raised his pistol for one last shot to end chuckles' life. i.dem.potent. asherah, habib, ma mère, shalom, seventy...blast! a bullet between chuckles' eyes. ha. son of asherah. the general picked up the bag and turned it inside out. hmm. he threw it aside. took a few glances around then noticed a few small figures watching him from the holes chuckles had punched into the wall. the homunculus scurried back into the dark hole. the general was sketched out and hurried to his feet to get back to the court.

☙

cal was bothered by **priniciples**. bobby said he would **pay** him **back** on friday. he realized how stupid it was to **lend** bobby money. what's this **unrelenting** stress, is this what an atom **feels** when it's being split? i'll go get a drink. a **couple** of minutes cal walked down the steps and **into** the pub. it was still early and there were only sook and jordan eno **inside**.
    calvin kale, sook said. hey. they shook hands. **THERE** hey, cal knodded to eno. eno looked away and started talking to sook again. before eno **IS** could even get a full word out cal cut him off. can i get a blonde please. when he looked over to **NOTHING** eno like, you can go on now. he was talking about the bassist in his band. i mean, he's a good **MORE** guy but he's always late and never follows what he did in rehersal. he say's he's fucking **THREATENING** rock and roll, the guy should learn how to play some rock and roll outside the cradle. he **TO** pissed as hell when i kicked him out. cal interrupted, did you ever think if rock and roll **THE** comes from the myth of sisyphus? i was wonderin. sook and eno were silent for a moment **ESTABLISHED** then laughed. oh man, what time is it? the sun's still out. smoke another one.
    was it the wrong time to say that? too early, **ORDER** not the right people? cal looked blankly back at the both of them. took a sip of his pint and **THAN** went outside to sit on the terrace. he saw a beautiful long legged girl in spandex walk by as

he **A** exited. damn, nice terrass. cal sat, rolled up a smoke, and looked through his bag. he took out **CRAZY** his note book and antonin artaud: correspondence avec jacques rivières. he couldn't **ARTICULATE** read. too many racing thoughts. the gravity was pressing him to the brink of an epiphany, **MUTT** he just had to endure.

i read in a language and notice the phrases yet lose myself in the slits of commas and pinholes of periods. lost in my own consciousness but awake in the symbols of the text event, cruxified between 't—t', crosshatched, interwoven by threads: latin and liberated from the terrorizing threat of moloch. the i-ron is the hybrid of my language, the absence of indigenous tongue. so the very nature of this french means: there is a forfeited ignorance inherent in it's use. the loss is recognized. then it's subversive to the established order, the existing design. so i adopt the orphan, the foreign bastard. move away from athens and claim a new citizenship. those greek mathematicians never got the zero concept. they moved along and built a universe without nothingness. cybernetic sha.mans jest and play behind the western text, through the implicit divisions of spaces, commas, periods. it's a liminal act, nomenclature fractured and fractal in no glory. the void bursts through the light in one giant storm, erasing the consummation of the self and allowing the multidimensional terrain to stitch and weave into a syntactic tapestry.

sook and eno came outside of the bar for a smoke. cal acted too involved in what he was doing to notice. he had to do something else, **¿WHOSE CIVILITY?** the writing wasn't fixing the problem the way it should of. he chugged back his pint, threw his books back into his bag. rushed off the patio. later guys.

    he had no idea where he was going. go look for mac? stop by edgars? where's bobby? busking? he took a left heading west down st.catherine. he hurried for half a block then stopped. naw, he turned back around and rushed back east. he got to the street corner and stood there. on the threshold of ideas and body. no confusion. both hemispheres. no **MORALITY** control over the other – he was existing in purgatory paradise. standing, watching what was happening beyond the traffic flow stopping and going at the intersection, through people, everyone with somewhere to go. it all streaming around. no time, no shift, no cycle, no bus, no appointment, no nothin. a moment of zen? then the key turned, aligning with the lock pins, off he went. he went to mac's and yelled his name from the street. nobody came to the window. he went to edgar's and rang the buzzer. there was no answer. he walked downtown to try and find bobby busking. he could be anywhere. maybe he was on the mountain.

cal walked up a few blocks to sherbrooke and cut through mcgill campus. fucked those kids up on frosh week. past ckut radio, ascending the streets till he got to the mountain's plateau. he'd been to bobby's camp site once and vaguely **ETHIC** remembered the trail to get there from the north east side. it was already eight thirty, dark would fall soon. cal had kept track of time but when he noticed the sun settin he figured he'd have a look anyway. he entered the woods of the mountain.

ꕥ

is everything under control down there general? yes your majesty, i have ordered agents to patrol the parameters. *you better make sure that nothing compromises our situation up here ever again. is that clear?*

yes your majestic reasonable sire sir. a tile of the floor in front of the reason's thrown popped up out of place. the general, reason and a few guards noticed. their eyes opened wide. w*hat the?* then all the fine black and white marble tiles began popping up chaotically. *they're here!* yelled reason. *they're here!* he lifted his feet onto the throne and held his arms around his legs.

the guards didn't know how to react. some of them were falling over. *attack*! the guards started smashing the floor with their swords and shooting with their guns. the giant chandelier in the middle of the court fell and crushed six agents. screaming and yelling and smashing and shooting and ching ching swords chopping.

come with me your majesty, this is not our fight. *take me to gravity! this is his undoing. it's all part of a bigger narrative! i can read that much. let's go!* the general picked up reason in his arms and they ran out of the court just as the homunculus began dropping on the soldiers, falling, uttering phonemes like rain drops. they fell through all the light fixtures and the chandelier's fixture. reason and the general paused and looked back in horror. *good messiah!* the tiny homunculus people were dropping down by the thousands. killing the guards with their pin swords in jugular veins, climbing up their noses, into their veins. the invisible fury. a massacre. a bloodbath. how the homunculus enjoyed it. murderous little bastards.

they slammed the door behind them and looked at each other. *why are you carrying me general?* i had to save you from danger, sire. *danger smanger. this is my palace, my kingdom, i will not back down.* how do we defeat what we cannot see sire? *oh, you can see them, you're just not close enough.* reason opened the door and kicked the general into the court. the homunculus ravaged the guards and agents. _____

they now **turned** their **attention to** the general. they advanced on him as a torrent of wind, piling up on top of each other, forming the shape of a **giant mouth**. fangs dripping homunculus back into the **shape**, cycling and gyrating life **movements**: the mouth **spoke** in a deep ominous howl and bellowed: **do you die for the sign?!**

the general took out his pistol and unloaded his clip. the bullets couldn't hit matter too small for ***conventional* destruction**. the general kept backing up until he was against the door. reason was on the other side. *your suffering will not be forgotten general.* the general pounded on the door, full of fear, he was going to be consumed and disembodied by the phonetic chatter of the fast approaching mouth that turned into the face of chuckles laughing and back to the giant mouth. he fizzled and discombobulated and was swallowed in one end and his skeleton shat out the other end. reason was on its way to the top of he tower to personally deal with gravity.

bobby stopped busking for the day

downtown, he **just** made seventy three **dollars** and eighty cents in six hours of busking. he hadn't forgotten **about** owing cal forty bucks and **planned** on **giving** him at least twenty back. **if** he saw him tonight. there weren't any **parties** that bobby **knew of** and he was wondering what the **night** would present. he'd been in the **middle** of a **song** when cal called earlier. he **was also** waitin to hear back from tina. she hadn't **responded** to any of his **messages** all week. the **sun** was setting and the sky burned **crimson** fluorescence over the city skyline. he'd get a **drink** he **thought** as he walked up **st.laurent street**. he walked into the most popular little shit hole on the main and **plunked** down in a chair **by** the windows. he could watch the **people** walk by. the waitress **came** up to his table **and gave** him **some** free popcorn in a red plastic chip tray. a pitcher of blonde please and thank you. sure he said. cheapest pitchers bobby knew of, ten **bucks**.
 who can **i** call? **who** can **i** call? he **tried** herring but **no** one picked up. **he tried** edgar but there **was** no answer. **why the fuck doesn't** cal have a phone yet. he texted his **avatar** crush. the waitress came back with the beer. that'll **be** ten dollars. here you **go**, sorry about the change. he **sifted through** pockets and made a pile of **change** on the table. that's okay, i **need** change for tonight. don't you like **it** when things work out **for** us **both** she wasn't having any of it. **could** have been all the change. she

walked **away** and bobby opened up the com**part**ment on his guitar **case** and took **out** even **more change**. he **divide**d it all into stacks. he was quite **pleased** with himself. a breeze came through **the** window. the **pool** table in the back cracked on a **break**, the waitress wiped **down** mugs and **banter**ed **with some** old drunks at the bar, the **music** was old school hip hop and the bulls played the pistons on the television over head.

☙

mac was at home playing his proper noise. it was the second last day of data collecting for his time capsule project.

some bellowing bastard's like no, gnaw means gnaw, there's too much to gnaw, no time to give digestion a break. would benefit from a fast. go on, echoin ghettos built up by the imagery of alien fabulas that taunt them till their memories are ghosts of words and their bodies have rotted in cheap caskets. rap away in simile and metaphor, rapping at death's door. honouring militants with carols saved for the x-mass. but the bellowing bastards wait for no gathering, x marks now, when they feel the earth shutter. hybrid monsters, cursed with artificial intelligence and an ego rush blown like failed matadors, the moor lingers. they halt and stand before the epaulette outlined figures of the red-flagged jewelers to sniff out tenderness in a cold stone. shallow discoveries are made, their spite has them laugh and scoff. only the revered will be spared, unless they too are found to contain cold rubies and diamonds for blood and spirit. the feigning species, sub-human, post-man, morbid dignity composts their fleshy love and shreds any trace of decency.

    the fool in them overshadows their lust, their palatable angst is intriguing and exotic to the exiled who collaborate with them. co-conspirators of the major arcana, marching by twenty twos, manifesting grit and teeth. superstition gets the better of them, they were informed by the lore of a law that was written through the lives of lost gospels. exodus sweeps them from day to day and only reconciliation is to quench ephemeral hunger-pains that burst out of their solar plexus;. just one drop has cased them into a spiraling conglomerate of zodiacs. the racial conditioning of your masters implores you still, my diaspora, the inferior race knows this, but you grip and grab like a baby for a tit, soothing the madness of your own dire longing.

  i'm sorry like a mother allows her children to eat her alive so they may live on. it's hard to dissuade the belief that we are in the midst of an astrological epidemic, under the same stars that the warriors of casamas used to guide them through the jungle and ambush arabian knights who evaded crusaders. the same stars that guided osiris to orion, the same that host the thirty six decans. i don't speak in vain, but in response to all that you neglect. mars or nergal of the underworld = what more could you expect but a fight to the death? no kingship would be auspicious enough to divert the awakening of this genealogical supremacy for all time.

  ibrahim, you doubling patriarch, a redemptive lion of judah was made in the vedas too. that's why socrates drank the hemlock, that's why philosophical heretics report from the shanghai world fair, that's why the 'pure' bred recite homer with a complacency that resembles a purring pussy. the dialogue goes on, the digestive track processes, fast or die little deaths with the cardinal force of the four seasons/gorge and face the big singular death that desires you. those same stars we learn more about with each passing day, let them not guide ya to zion, occupy babylon with all your confusion and refusals and pathologies, learn them well and you will walk again.

☙

cal walked into **the forest**. there was fifteen minutes of sunlight **left**, twenty max. a flock of birds flew out of the tree canopies and fluttered the leaves. cal watched for a moment as the small birds flew like a **single** *organism*, the underside of their wings shimmered like a handful of nickels thrown into the air. heads or tails, the **coordinates** never stop. **self governing-dynamics**.

   he stepped into the shade and took **the path** he thought led him to bobby's camp spot. a few massive boulders **with graff** tags sprayed on them, or were they hobo warnings? he **remembered** them. keep on going. **a** right? the **fork** in the path. shit. ye. **no**, no, there wasn't **a** log **bridge**. fuck this, i don't know where the fuck i'm goin, it's **already dark**. he heard some people walking about one hundred meters away. how the fuck does bobby **do** this every **night**, drunk as a mutherfucker? maybe its through here **actually**. cal remembered you had to leave the **trail and** cut through **heavy** bush and poison ivy. ugh. bobby!? he yelled. **you there**? bobby?!

   the people **he heard** talking were walking past him now. a middle aged guy and **a slightly** younger girl, both of them **handsome** and dressed in fresh hiking shoes, **grey** and yellow breathable active wear type shit. hi, said bobby. the girl smiled and they kept on walking, the man **display**ing defensive **instincts**. my woman. we walk **through** this **land** in peace. **guess** he didn't get his rocks off at the top of the mountain. cal would of **left right** away but he didn't want to follow directly **behind** the couple. he rolled **a smoke**. now he looked weird just standing off the **trail** smoking by himself, single tanned male, sketched out glance, someone would thing he was a weirdo.

   okay, just follow them casually, who cares, nobody wants to be here by themselves once the sun goes down. maybe a fire. fuck well i dunno, cal was wandering aimlessly into the open field, the blades of grass blue green in static. he vaguely recalled something about elves and glanced around, just some folks throwing a lit up frisbee, a few dog walkers, horns honking down parc avenue. he smoked fast and rolled another cigarette. could sure go for a joint. i'll go use the internet. he wandered up parc, past the greek restaurants, up into mile end. he could of sworn there was an internet spot around there. he remembered walking by on on occasion. but he never went in. walking. walking. back down parc, the valets were busy, a bentley, ballers. he walked past a crew of hip kids he recognized but never spoke to, just familiar faces. he stepped into a small arabic dep that sold nothing but chips, beer, cigarettes and big bags of rice. he bought a can of beer and cracked it open before he even stepped out of the store. the clerk said something but cal just kept on walking.

joe

bobby poured the last of his pitcher into this glass. bobby, someone said leaning in on the window. hey man, whats up? it was joseph, another kid from toronto. nothin much man, just picked up some psylicibin fungi. is that so, bobby sounded curiously. you wanna pop some. um. i was just going to have a few beers but what else do i have to do. okay. stick around for a drink while i finish mine though. bobby got up and walked out front where joseph was. he lit a smoke and drank quickly.

    can i see them? are they **any good**? not here man, but ye, they **supercallafrajalistic** shit mang. **blue** caps the size of a loonie. dayum. okay, i'm comin. you want this? sure. bobby passed joe his cig. he went inside, chugged his beer, picked up his guitar and off they went up st.laurent.

    the streets were **crowded** with club kids, a couple mooks, lots of cops, some squeegee kids there was an MMA fight **being** broadcasted at the sports bars. they **bustled down** the **blocks**, lookin at the girls, the cars, the window shops. where do you wanna go? i dunno, how bout the **mountain**?

    sure. oh shit, look who it is. mr. cal kale. it's my buddy over there standin **at the corner**. how much **mush** do you have? **enough** to go around. i'll **treat** him. bobby cawed from the across **the** street. cal snapped out of a **daze** and spotted bobby and joe. **the light turned green**. he crossed towards them. what's up guys. pounds. pounds. cal, joe, joe, cal. just who i was lookin for. well here i am, **whatchya** sayin cal kale. i'm broke yo, you wouldn't happen to have some **cash** for me would you? i can give **you twenty**. shit, but joe here's got a **back** of mushroom **eucharist**s and we're goin to the mountain. you **down**? sure but i don't want any shrooms, i'll take **that** twenty though. okay. you sure? you goin to be **missin out**. ya. alight then. shit. i'll buy you a forty.

reason vs. gravity

reason burst into the stochastic chamber at the top of the tower. second-in-**command** was playing chess **against** one of the agents. *what **the blood** is going on here?!* second-in-command and the agent jumped **from** their chairs and knocked **the** table over. the chess pieces flew and clunked on the **floor**. *i'm sorry to disturb your game second-in-command, but we are being invaded, the general is dead and why isn't gravity storytelling!!!???* he is sir. *you fool! haven't you been listening to him? he's made all of this happen. damnit! and you agent, jump out of the window! um... do it! yes your majestic reason sire.* **the agent climbed** up **onto** the window sill and looked back. *JUMP!* ahhhhhhhh. the agent jumped to his **death**.

    gravity was still being suspended, quietly mouthing **the words** to the narrative. *look, second-in-command. listen! do you understand the words that are coming out of his mouth?* n.n.no your reason. reason walked over **to** gravity and slapped him in **the face**. *storyteller! who put you up to this?! why have you forsaken me?! did i not provide for you? shelter you? nourish you? answer me storyteller!*

        uh, uh, the storyteller was weak and tired. *oh, this isn't right, this is not just.* he violently turned to second-in-command. *how could you think everything was going to be fine, this propitious recanting that you imagined was happening may have cost us the war.* sir, sire, the general is dead? reason slapped him across the face. *yes you insolent oaf...there was nothing i could do to save him.*

    second-in-command, you negligence is inexcusable. guards, apprehend him! but sire. *but but but nothing. throw him out the window.* yes your logical reason. the guards grabbed second-in-command by the arms and dragged him to the window. please, sire, i'll do anything, i'll suck your dick, i'll be your slave. *second-in-command, you are my slave, or that is, you were.* and out the window he was thrown. reason listened until the screaming was inaudible and ended.

    guards, leave us alone for a moment please. **the four guards** shuffled out of the chamber. reason was looking at the floor and sighed. he raised his head slightly and turned to **look at gravity** through the corner of his eye.

---

are you aware of the bedlam that is unraveling down in the palace, storyteller? you must be. did you know it would happen like this? i had heard of the stories when i was a child. reason reminisced and smiled fondly. your father was an excellent story teller, you learned from the best. i always remember when he took me to sit upon his knee and he told me a story about a woman who cared for the land and cared for the sea. the thought of someone so capable and benevolent, loving and nurturing, i imagined what it would be like to have a mother like that. my father told me my mother was a whore who fornicated with a neighbouring king. she never came back because she would have been killed. i hated her with all my will. storyteller. do you understand?

gravity just listened. *i blamed my bitch of a mother for my weaknesses and faults. she became the justified means to an end, to my totality as the ruling ideal. so i have built this empire solely from the supreme sublimation i was provided with. extravagance. industry. abundance. but all this has been modified under one condition. what is it that i value most? totality itself? but what is this totality if i cannot know it all? what what i want to know is what is best for the continuity of the sublime i cherish so. if i know most of all what sublime then i myself must possess some essence of its power. to know, storyteller, is what i never have fully committed myself to, i realize, because....i don't know my mother. i never sought to ever ask which king she eloped with. i shouldn't blame father. it was enough to see how much my father hated her, despised her for what she had done to him, to me, and the entire kingdom. he had always assured me that we were better off without her and attested to this verity by providing me with all authenticity that was unique and rare, the finest things one could possess, all so that i could experience the multitudes of one singular certainty and that i know how to judge* *the difference. it was immediate. i was born into it and would know first hand. but in the back of my mind, as i grew, i recognised how many hands experience had actually passed through before it got to me. was it second hand, third hand, fourth hand? i was never in the position to put things off until later, everything passed through me and everyone else in the kingdom was to wait. it was the rational logic of my role. i had my reasons, didn't i? should i not represent all that the kingdom should aspire to, that is, all besides me?*

---

reason was reasonably **shook**. there was the pressure of populations **on** his soul, **weighing** on it's **consciousness, enough to** crush him like an egg if he lost his **balance**. it was **true** that **gravity** and **reason** had grown up **together**, they used to **play** together **as** children. but **one** day gravity had **accidentally seen something** he shouldn't of. **and since** then **he knew** what **he** had to do. it **was** the eve of reason senior's third **evolution**. **he was** in his **quarter**s writing a **critique** of beezlebub's influence on the **lumpen** proletariat. gravity and reason jr. were playing chess. junior hadn't been **focus**ed the entire evening. he kept on checking the **time**. gravity, **as** gravities have **the ability to intuit**, sensed junior was **waiting for something**. junior said he had to **go** to the bathroom **and** would fetch a snack in the kitchen for the two of them. he **excus**ed himself and walked out of **the game** room. gravity waited a moment then followed him. he **look**ed **down** the hall but junior wasn't **there**.

he **look**ed **the other way** and saw juniors **shadow turning** the corner. the kitchen **or** the bathroom weren't in **that** direction. he was heading for **reason** senior's quarters. gravity tiptoed around **the corner** and saw junior **in** front of **the door** of this father's chamber. he **was preparing a vial** and stashed it up his sleeve. he then **knock**ed on the chamber door and his father **greet**ed him **in**. they discussed the **festivities for** his father's third evolution celebrations the **next day**. then junior **ask**ed his father **if** he was **thirsty? would** he like to have a pre-celebratory toast?

gravity watched through the keyhole as junior prepared two drinks, one had been **mix**ed with **the contents** of the vile junior had up his sleeve. that night **reason** senior **died of a messy death**, he was **found** the next morning, **suffocated by** a rare **case** of perverse **reverse**. a sick form a constipation. he had choked to death on his own excrement.

 it was **ugly**, shit was **found** dribbling from his mouth as **his corpse** hung off the bed. he **clear**ly made an **attempt to** shit it out of his mouth but ran out of oxygen before he could **succeed**. junior was **proclaim**ed the **new** ruler of reason and reigned until the present **day**.

 reasonable **logic was** his father's murderer, **a hater** of mothers, an **all around** troubled individual. **gravity** had no sympathy for him. it was rather **tragic**, but still. of all **potions** to die from.

 reason walked up **face to face** with gravity, suspended **in space**, he exhaled **loud** and sensual and wiped a single bead of sweat off of gravity's brow. *guards!* the guards came shuffling back in. *release gravity from the stochastic device* he said as he cooly walked away and turned to the **window**. looking out upon **the kingdom that was** unaware of what was **happening behind** the palace walls. **the storyteller** was **released** and fell to the cold stone floor. he was weak and struggled to support **himself**. what do you want from me? he raised to one knee. *there's something i believe you know gravity, and i want you to tell me. what do the ends mean?*

pre.meditations

cal, bobby and joe walked out of a dep. cal had a forty that bobby bought for him and the other two bought candy and orange juice. the small and narrow street was quiet compared to the saturday night circus that was beginning on st.laurent. joe took out the plastic ziplock bag and gave half a handful of its contents to bobby. your flesh of god my friend. really? damn boi, thanks (there was more than he bargained for). he ate a few pieces at a time and cringed. you got to chew it for a while to get the most out of em, said joe. joe took a handful and shoved them all in his mouth. the saliva activates the psylicibin. fuck, pass me the juice. tastes like shit, yaauuuck. bobby shook it off. joe was still chewing. it's not that bad man, he said with his mouth full. cal looked on with little interest. what's wrong man? here, i swear this is medicine man. bobby handed cal a mushroom cap. just take like point two grams, this piece. microdosing is the future from the past. the best anti-depressant anti-anxiety make you feel good shit on the market mang. cal looked up at bobby's eyes. i'm fine though, i'm not depressed and shit. there's something sorting itself out in my head, i can't figure it all out yet, i can't see it all at once. but it's there. this can help that too mang! bobby was excited. cal put the cap in his mouth and chewed for 10 seconds then swallowed. he twisted his forty open and said cheers and took back a slug.

 they walked up to the same path cal was at earlier. i knew it was this way. i couldn't remember where to go. don't fret my friend. you got any joints? joe had. can i buy a dime off you? sure. cal looked at joe insistently. now? we'll wait till we sit down, burn, then the shrooms'll start to kick in hey boys, pick up any firewood you see. i can't see anything. joe took out his cellphone and used the light from the screen. bobby took a head lamp out of this guitar case. amateurs. i was a boy scout you know. be prepared they said.

༄

the three of them trampled through the brush and picked up enough wood to start a fire. bobby already had some good fuel layin around. i can't believe you've been sleepin here for a month. nothins gone wrong. ye, knock on wood. are you sure it's cool we have a fire here? asked joe. ya mahn, i've checked, you can't see anything from anywhere. it took them a bit but they eventually got a fire going and joe flipped cal a dime. they passed the joint around and the two's trip started.

 oh ho, shit, fuck, fuuuuck, haha. two hours later and life was blaring. fuck, who woulda thought you could have a campfire in the middle of montreal eh? on dis here royal mountain i can't say anything because it's just like, i say the same shit over, you know, just saying things to explain something else that needs to be explained by someone else for someone else….you see what i mean. bahaha. fuckin solipsisms. what? psylisybin solipsisms maaaan, hahaha! these things are the most satirical drug of them all! whoa!! mycelium thought waves. transmitting…is anyone out there hahaha

༄

man, i remember this one time, me and some friends went to my buddy's cottage. it was on an island right. i brought four grams of mush. i don't know why i didn't bring more. motherfuckers bought a keg between six or seven of em. shit. i ate two in the afternoon and didn't really catch. just floatin in the river, starin at the clouds. so i popped the other two a few hours later. i was gooone. man, they were all inside playing poker, yelling at each other cuz fifty bucks went missing. i was just sittin outside man, by the fire, like this. i had one beer the whole night. every sip was like an electric shock through my entire nervous system. i was vibrating out of my fuckin mind. starin at the fire, laughin, talkin to the trees, it was fucked…pffff

 ahahaha! shit. this one time we took some powdered, bottom of the bag type shit, mixed with chocolate. we were drivin around the outskirts of town…you were drivin?

 ya mahn, and we pull down this dirt road to smoke a joint, it was just getting dark, you know. and we got the car parked and there's this light that appears out of nowhere. like two hundred meters in front of us. and it's getting bigger and bigger. i'm fuckin lookin up at the sky looking for some fuckin u.f.o. or something. fuck, i got up ready to jump in the car and peel out, i was trippin. turned out it was headlights on the trees, i couldn't tell, then a car turned the corner. scariest fifteen seconds of my life man.

༄

this shit man, it brings out the elements of life. clear as day. i was on em, one friend had been sniffin blow, the others were just smoking joints. i saw the fuckin devil in my friends face. the one blitzed on yayo. maybe cuz i was the only one who knew he was high. he'd turn and look at me, enticing me to take a line, the other guys were all docile and stoned like sacred cows.

☙

another time i saw, man, i mean like, humanity, what it thought i should have. i had my girl, a pocket full of cash, a big growler of brew, my trailer, cuz everyone else was sleepin outside in tents, my consciousness, you know, like that's all that mattered, if i had all those things my life was complete. i was the man. but what the fuck does that mean when i'm dead? you lived a good life. it's somethin to be. you live to support life and what's good about it. that's all u can do. is it? what else is bigger than that? i dunno, science and shit. why don't you enlighten me? hahaha

cal just sat there and listened, he'd finished his forty and was rollin a joint. cal, man, bobby cracked up. how you feelin over there. fine man, enjoyin the fire. word man. it ain't bad eh?! here. the joint was passed. what else is goin on tonight? i wanna go to the bar, bobby said. i don't know if i could handle that man. you just put our sunglasses on and dive in man. it's fun. the things you can do. oh man. you can travel through time man. like an elastic, you're a siamese twin and one wants to go one way and the other wants to go the other way, eventually, the both of you are pullin and stretchin that skin in between you till it snaps you both back to some spot neither one of you were tryin to get to, but you both end up there and you gotta decide if you're goin to compromise and work together, go home, walk together or try to go your own separate ways again. i prefer the last way. i like surprise landings.

how is that time travel? man, look at it like this, you're a circus freak, your parents loved you but it's the only work the both of you can get, you and your siamese twin. you ever been to siam? no, but that's what they call you, the both of you, siamese twins. in that moment, the moment people pay to see you, the bearded lady, the strong man, the leprechaun, no matter where you're from, they're paying to see siamese motherfuckin twins man. your connected at the hip, your oppositional identity. like the elephant man or the tree man, the elephant and the man, the fungus that looks like bark and the man behind it all. they make freaks out of all of us man, me and my motherfuckin problems. who's to say i got problems? who's to say i don't? i'm not tryin to make enemies, but my "problems" are made into enemies, enemies of the muthafuckin state man. they gotta fill that space and use it for somethin, that void, and you damn well better believe that the problem of the enemy is an enemy because it's a conflict of interest, of power, total power! do you understand what i'm talkin about, can you overstand this shit?! bobby was standing up, waving his hands in the air again, the fire glowing on his face, in a trance, falling into the cyclical pattern of dying words for newborn words and dead words all over again. the unoccupied space kills. the fear. the hate. the ignorance. they can't stand it, but the only way to fix the problem is to fight fire with fire. but their fire is real. there is no fire. fuckin greeks man, babylon's got no zero, no return, they don't think of it, progress, progress, build...build!

 okay okay, joe looked at cal laughing. this guy wants to go to the bar? bobby kept on going. they want my problems, they can have them, kill them, torture them, my cancer, my pancreas, my delusions, my black lung, it's one or the other! my body or my problems, can't control em both. that's even against their law.

 here man, have a cig, calm down, please, said cal. bobby looked at cal blankly then snapped out of his rant. he laughed, mad and young. am i out of control? i wouldn't say so. you're just fuckin screamin like a maniac. sorry sorry. **whoa! lol.**

 you guys wanna go to the bar now? i wanna go walk around at least, said joe. okay, let's do this. bobby was an intensity of refracted light, a quipo code on fire, just bridging the flame with another string, another de/re.coded picture show of the mosaical montage, burning the bridge behind him and all that was before it just to remember the stories and make a game from code to bridge to string to string over and over again. distant memories were captured in his myth making oratory. he would burn and burn until he ran out of string and forget how he got to where it was he had settled. he kept on with his myths but burned bridges no more. it wasn't the time, or was it just not this place? who's to say? who's willing to find out? a clean break.

cal didn't move. hey man, you comin? naw, cal stared into the fire, i'm goin to sit with the fire. bobby didn't hesitate, okay man, see you later. there's a sleeping bag in this tree, and an extra flashlight. okay man, thanks. word. peace yo. bobby grabbed his guitar. peace. bobby and joe walked out of the forest, down the hill and into the city. what's the deal with buddy? nothin, he's thinkin is all. sees better in the dark. what? nevermind.

ဢ

gravity sat in a chair, fully clothed again, with guards on either side of him. reason was still looking out the window. he leaned down and picked up a pawn that had fallen from earlier. he examined the piece. *the pawn*, he stated, *has nowhere to go but forward, one space at a time, except for its initial move where it may be allowed to advance two coordinates ahead. only if the pawn succeeds in killing an opposing piece may it move diagonally. you've been playing in the king's court for some time now, storyteller, have you been an outpost? isolated? too far advanced, left with no defense? it would appear as though you have gone rogue, i can't tell if you're playing for black or for white. did you actually think you could contend against me? that nobody would notice you? it was your life or mine, storyteller, but what would it matter. well surely the kingdom would grieve the loss of their majesty, who would grieve for you? you have no family, no friends, your sole purpose was to tell stories for me and my court. ah yes, but you did love, didn't you, once, your fair e.m. the shape shifting bitch she was. it wasn't easy containing her. i heard she put up quite the fight. i've made a humpty dumpty out of her, but my men know to not even bother putting her back together again. and so i ask one more time, and you will answer me, storyteller, what do the ends mean? and what differs between mine and yours if not only a death of two different bodies?* gravity looked back into dandy reason's eyes and said nothing. *speak! damn you storyteller! and now you will not speak to save your life after all the evolutions?!*

here we are, reason, in the tower. your palace, down there, being deconstructed brick by brick, pillar by pillar, and you ask me, the low storyteller, for an answer to a question i've never thought of myself. and this time, to think you've never really understood my stories, that you listened to them because of they were pleasing to you? because they satisfied your ego? or did you know how to listen? reason snickered to cover his preposterous guilt. i know this much, your majesty, i know you are one of the children of asherah. gravity stood up. the guards put their hands on his shoulders to push him back down but reason waved his hand to let him be. reason's jaw tightened, he turned his face away from gravity in disgust. gravity took slow measured strides towards reason. yes reason, your father denied this too. he never wanted to accept that asherah was not meant solely for him and him alone. no! i have no mother! your mother is asherah, your majesty. *it can't be true*, said reason looking up at the ceiling. gravity advanced with force in his step, pushed reason out of the way and jumped onto the window sill. *huh?* you can't win em all. *get him!* the guards rushed. gravity jumped. logic got up and cleared the way to the window. what? the storyteller dissipated, evaporated, dematerialized into the colour of the air. where did he go?

then a faint sound like the buzzing of a fly was heard. reason's attention was fixed and sharpened, uncertain. he was baffled. the noise got louder and more articulated. it rose up from the bottom of the tower. reason looked out the window and couldn't believe his eyes as the ruins of his palace were settling and the dust made a sweeping cloud. the cloud kept on rising up the side of the tower walls. the tower walls trembled. the articulation rose with dust and began to howl and scream and wail sonic mayhem. it was the same noise that came from the forest. reason collapsed to his knees, screaming, he covered his ears in agony. the guards were unsure of what to do. one looked out the window. the force of the howling was so close and powerful it knocked him off his feet and into reason. reason and the guard were on the floor, the other guards ran out of the door. the entire tower was in a tornado of dust and howls. homunculus clung to the agents and reason and pop. they all became phonemes of idempotency, inhaled into the process of the fractal usurper. an abrupt ending. then the homunculus phonemes turned and looked at you.. hello. yes, you. grinning.

&

cal had kept quiet while the other two were there. grandma always said, if you don't have anything nice to say don't say anything at all. but what if you think bad things? cal could of got up and left or told the two to shut the fuck up, but he didn't, he waited to be alone with the fire, it was just his irrational desiring ego that perceived displeasure in loss of control. there was no need to be like that, there was no one that wanted that.

now he sat in front of the fire in the forest on mount royal. he couldn't hear the streets, he couldn't hear the stereo systems pumping out of the clubs, the horns honking, the drunks yelling, bobby yelling for that matter, he had a little sanctuary, a space to reflect and sort out the language of his thoughts that had been increasing in rates of ideas x the images ÷ by his ego^3. it'd become daunting.

he flipped through his notebook and looked back on his scribblin that seemed to be like clues left by a scribe from a thousand years ago. if only they hadn't of lost those texts in the razing of the grand temple at sakhara, the library of alexandria or in wa'set. he looked at the words that he had written and stared into the flames. one thought thrown into the flame, he watched it jump and curl. it moved in tongues with non specific amplification that momentarily blinded the eyes and deafened the ear like a flash grenade. but they didn't control his experience. he had the cognitive liberty to let his mind manifest itself with the feedback play that excreted out of the dialogue. there were no things to get in the way besides himself. the words were telescopes into constellations of his morphological synthesis. constantly regathering and remapping, territorializing, deterritorializing, reterritorializing like a nomad on an illusive flight through biographic planes. words like messianic noumenon. words like transcendental scintilla like etymological derivatives of psychedelic doxa like iboga serum like siddartha's entelechy like aubsane prophets unlike poxied words of uncritical negritude in garveyite accelerationism like methodological scapegoat like aztec eucharist like shaman's pharmacopeia like tangible synaesthesia unlike proto-fascist hyperlinks.

 i think i am, but who am i and where is here? i've never really been convinced. a pristine defeat is enough to trigger the euphoria you feel before starving to death. like undifferentiated experience, non-teleological sine waves, libidinal inertia, questi-on reflex. hermetic anatomy of the afro-trash bastard in acousmatic rhizomes, the infinite digression for holistic serenity, freudian slips in the space-time continuum, diplozygoti spirals of voodoo, geotrauma, ecliptic ovulocycle, lexicography in two hundred fifty six bit, tetragrammatron. rastafarian kabbalah, the theosophical fallacy of a hip hop gospel like extra sensory perception prophesizing your parent's wardrobe as i believe in you when it doesn't matter because we all lead different paths in the same direction like schismogenesis rupturing from a racialized object as an idea like ethnic cleansing of the capitalist spectacle like stan o'neil thought about the children as michelle jean was the prototype for obama like that's why there's more and more british news anchors on cnn like anachronistic antagonistic time travellers as grandma looks through the photo album like jean toomer was into gurdjieff before the war on drugs failed as antidepressants and antipsychotic sales multiplied by fifty fold within twenty years like we're all so sad and only getting crazier as das kapital gave up searching for zion when the all seeing eye was trusted in the bonds of the words that were conscripted in constitutions and emancipations and proclamations, designations, modifications, adaptations, saturations, alienations and ations of sations we don't question like when the state triumphed as we were made to forget our irreducibility like aesthetics did for god like the church and the pope's gold cross unlike humans aren't just one species as a panacea like european positivism like wittgenstein the assassin a creator as individual for they schools?

    i have no idea what time it is and there's only, there's no more fire wood. let this burn out. no. fuck it. cal kicked dirt over the fire and figured it must of been two or three o'clock. he flicked on the flashlight and traipsed through the bush onto the trail. he thought he heard food stops comin up behind him. he swung around. there was nothing there besides the trees. he walked fast down the trail now, slipped and cut his ankle but kept on going fast till he got out of the forest and into the open field of the mountain plateau.

    he had to catch the night bus at atwater so that he could make it all the way back up to côte-vertu in the north end. he went back down into town, cut through mcgill campus and headed across the downtown club scene. mini skirts and ginos. he went to the pub to try and get a last-call drink but the door was locked. he walked, rushed to catch a bus he didn't know when it would show. he had to wait half an hour. not bad. he went to the internet spot to check his email.

    when he got back he thought. catch the transfer from vendôme. get back up town by five thirty, six o'clock. no way in hell i'm goin to work. can't be fucked. nuh uh. it's all goin to happen, it is happening, this event, this life. the process. can't be blocked. remove excess to get through more. alethia. can't be stopped. won't stop. he rolled a cig and sat down on the bench in front of the same park bobby was arrested in. psychic footprints. who else has been here? blood in the earth grew back up and gave life a second chance.

    bert rolled by on his bike. hey man do you have an extra smoke? no. he kept on going and stopped at the payphones where the strange duo of a forty somethin year old white lady and the no more than twenty five year old black dude had been hangin around. cal watched bert go and come back then leave with the white girl then comeback after the black kid disappeared then he came back and then the three of them left together. then the bus came.

    when cal got to vendôme he realized he forgot his notebook with his book bag at the fire. a copy of the human comedy, but his notebook! what was in it? notes, he'd had that book for three months. three months worth of ideas gone, m.i.a like prison. he had written his freedom and now it was taken away like a child he was to unfit to parent. he contemplated going back. he paced back and forth on the sidewalk in front of the metro stop. he cursed himself out loud. fuckin shit, you fuck, god damnit, no, i'll be alright, it'll be there, bobby'll see it, but what if he doesn't and some…naw, who's walkin around in the bush at this time. it'll be light soon though. but still, naw, nobody, i wonder if bobby went back? who knows what debauchery they got into. cot damnit.

    he sat down and rolled a smoke. his knee bounced up and down. the nervous energy was pulsing in the back of his neck, the medulla oblongata to the pyramids. he felt the electricity from his toes to the motor fibres. his synaptic regimes were in rapid fire. he scoured his memory to think of the most critical bits of writing he'd noted. about being left lust-fucked by maggie, lame and self-depricating, he recalled. he wrote a sociological formula to suggest and predict the various epistemological applications of pop culture cross-breeding through various genres and mediums. that was somethin he'd have troubles doing over. a few rough poems. the newspaper delivery van came by and threw a stack down in front of the metro doors. then the bus came. he got on and sat in the back. he took a pen from his pocket and realized that he never paid joe for the dime that he got off him. he didn't have any paper so he started jottin down words on his arm because he wished he was wearing long sleeves.

i was pacing then tripped on a fissure and a holiday sky eclipsed
i went down and saw the top multiple the bottom. how else could i explain what was happening?
then i thought, did that pull together?
a break from this tension would be nice. it ain't right either
marching left, right, left, right...
they symbols are the earth's will
and these days we're never that far away from any way.
stretches and calisthenics in a current's drift to
irregulate and erode the bank
of my shores.
i'll send postcards in our decorded and exiled words so you can:
my translated heartbeat and body. i'll enjoy pacing,
between here and somewhere,
half uncertain, half noxious,
half thankful,
half way.

☙

he was the only person on the bus. the pale blue light of dawn was moving over the night sky. the moon was still visible. cal looked out the window as the bus made its way along décarie blvd. it was sunday morning. the twilight of insomnia wasn't buzzing yet. cal's pupils were dilated and he was refusing to believe this is what enlightenment felt like. he knew it wasn't that because he couldn't get the forgotten book out of his mind. what were those words? the buzz had cal wide awake, the effects of the alcohol he drank earlier had long ago faded. he thought. gazed. looked through. perceived. leviathan was at the tip of his tongue like an immortal technique. for a moment he felt like he was ready to die. as prepared as he could ever be for his final judgement, a few extra words weren't going to change the sentence. he was a zealot in transit, the lone fool on this bus that would shuttle him to another terminus where he would catch another bus. would h ever get home? he wasn't alone against a logos that claimed no contrary, he knew that, but where was everybody? they're asleep, he told himself, or waking up to go to work, or dancing at an after hours with everyone else inducted into the dance manifesto. the past few weeks had incited a total abandonment from just causes and the self, he forgot about accomplishment, his actions had no motivation, he was a machine at war against an opponent he couldn't separate from his body, it was the life support that he couldn't tolerate anymore. the raw quid pro quo. made it all seem so violent like the scent of blood does to the most vicious predator. but he knew better, no matter what form the blood bait took, he wouldn't take it.

    it was a game, he was a player, a body that couldn't be assembled without being feared, hated, demonized, persecuted or at the least, imprisoned, he'd come to learn this through some bastardized incapacity to accept what he saw.

    the bus finally got to côte-vertu. he had to transfer one more time. the bus would be there in a few minutes. when it arrived he had to argue with the bus driver. the driver tried to make him pay because his transfer had expired. it wasn't cal's problem the buses didn't get him to where he need to be going on time. if that's the problem, deal with it. when they got to his stop he went up to the front of the bus and stood beside the bus driver to make sure he didn't purposefully go by his stop because they had an argument. miserable man.

    cal walked right up to the front door of his grandma's old folks home and stood still. he checked himself. he was wide awake. he wanted to get his notebook back. what was he going to do at his grandmother's anyway? sleep the day away? no. the notebook. cal turned around and walked back to the metro, it was early, the sun was out, vitamins like no other. once he got there he remembered to call and leave a message at work to say that he wouldn't be able to make it in today. the stm toll booth worker must have been in the bathroom or something because there was no one there to buy a ticket. he jumped the turnstile and made his way back downtown. it was about that time that cal would be makin his way to work if he was going to work, he was liable to see other employees on the metro too. he sat in the first car to avoid being seen.

    he took the longer metro ride to mount royal and walked to the mountain. there were people on the mountain enjoyin the early sun vibes. no tam tams yet. he went up the trail that led him to the fire spot. cut through the brush. his bag was gone, the notebook wasn't there either. cal looked around and tried to determine what had gone on here in the past few hours. he felt like he had a heightened sense of awareness that would allow him to intuit what the environment had to say. the fire pot was wet. he dabbed it with his pinky and smelled. urine. yughck. he wiped it off on his pant leg. he looked up to the tree where the sleeping bag was. it was still there. he looked around the other trees knowing that bobby had his duffle bag hidden in another one. he looked at the footprints. he couldn't recall what kind of shoes joe was wearing but the sandal imprints of bobby and another set were prominently evident where they both were sittin last night.

    cal saw the pine tree branch that bobby used to sweep the floor before he would leave. this would clean the tracks away and let bobby know if anyone had been there while he was gone. why didn't you sweep before you left cal? there was also evidence of spit on the dirt. there was a fourth set of footprints. only a few, that walked straight through the campsite, took a piss, picked up the bag, spat and into the bush.

    what the fuck? he followed the footsteps to where it looked like they went right into thick viney brush. cal marched right in with his arms above his head. to avoid getting tangled and cut on thorns. this person must of known exactly where they were going he thought. there was a trail wide that looked to be used by cars just up ahead. no sign of the bag to the left, no sign to the right as he trudged on. he got to the clearing for the road by surprise and slipped down the short fall in the rocks. brushed and patted the dust off his clothes. now what? where? maybe bobby had the bag. he had to get to a payphone.

fifteen minutes later. bobby's phone must be dead. cal headed to the internet spot. he passed one of the seediest bars downtown and saw an old timer sittin at the window with a pitcher of beer to himself. good mornin good guiness, or whatever the poor guy was drinkin. he hopped up the grimey steps of the internet cafe and used his shit to turn the door knob. half an hour of time please. you come offin, the clerk said. why you no buy membaship? save money.

not today. next week. payday. oh, haha, okeh. cal put a toonie on the counter. numba thirty three. thanks. checked his email. nothin. he logged into facebook and sent bobby a message. where u @? dun appen a ave my book bag do u? he spent the next half an hour looking at status updates and pictures. edgar was waking up with rebecca by his side. he paid for another hour after that toonie ran out.

the morning after

edgar was waking up with rebecca by his side. the sly dog had his first real date with her the night before. the whole shabang. dinner at an italian restaurant, the movies, drinks at a bar with live music. at the end of the night he said you can sleep at my house if you want. done. good morning. hi, she said stretching out and smiling. a little kiss. too polite to tongue without brushing their teeth. did you sleep well? asked edgar. ya. i had a dream that i was hiking up a mountain. somewhere tropical. with a guide that spoke in spanish. and my best friend from high school was with me. then we got to this plateau and there was a waterfall and i swam behind the waterfall and found a panda bear. the panda spoke to me in spanish too. he told me to beware of the guide, because sometimes he lied. so me and my friend ditched the guide and shared our food with the panda bear. spanish pandas eh? laughed edgar. do you speak spanish. un poquito.

i hardly ever remember my dreams but i know i have them. they say you'd go crazy if you didn't dream. i've heard that before too. i imagined it would be like waking up from death if there wasn't an after life. really? that's kind of creepy, she giggled. i gotta go to the bathroom before i think anymore. ya me too. okay, go first. do you drink coffee? i love coffee. okay, i'll put some on. they both got out of bed and got dressed. checking themselves out. it was the first time they were sober to see each other naked. if you want there's a fresh towel in the bathroom if you want to shower. ya, i feel like i need to shower. okay, i'll just take a quick piss. he pissed.

edgar was in the kitchen and started a batch of coffee. he looked through the cupboards and fridge but there wasn't much to eat for breakfast. rice, mustard, salt. he spent almost all his money last night. he went to the living room and felt light on his toes. he hadn't gotten laid in months. he sat down on the couch and exhaled with satisfaction. he started up the computer and played leonard cohen, songs from a room.

☙

rebecca walked into the living room after her shower. feeling fresh? ya, i feel great. i just want to say i had a good time last night. ya, me to. edgar got up and they kissed. how bout some coffee? please. coming right up. i love leonard cohen. is this the album. indeed it is edgar said from the kitchen. that band last night did a cover of this song. he came back with the coffee, cream and sugar. thanks. really? i didn't notice. ya, it was a little later on, i think we already had two or three drinks by that point, plus the bottle of wine at dinner. they both laughed.

what are you up to today? asked rebecca. well i've gotta go to the library and finish a paper. it's already a few weeks late, i have to have it in by tomorrow or i fail. but it's no problem, i'm almost done. i wanna get working soon kinda, so i don't have to waste the day in the library. it's too nice outside. not that i'm kickin you out or anything. lol. oh that's okay, i'm supposed to meet my dad for brunch. soon anyway. what's cool. she had a couple sips from her cup and put down on the table. she looked at the time on the computer. i'm actually going to be late. i better go now. oh. alright then. they kissed one more time. call me again soon, she said. i'll be doing that, edgar replied. have a nice day. you too, good luck with your paper. thanks. she gathered her purse, slipped on her shoes and went out the door smiling. edgar went back to the computer and got a message from cal. got any janja? ya mahn. enuf to front a dime? i guess so. thanks man. r u home? leavin soon. meet @ library. third floor. word. cheers. a+. a+. he folded his laptop shut and went into the bathroom to brush his teeth. got properly dressed. eye out a dime on the coffee table and wrapped in aluminum foil. his notebooks and other books. threw them in his book bag. stood up in the middle of the living room and scanned like sonar to check if he was forgetting something. it didn't feel like it. out the door he went. stepped outside. the sun was shining. he had that extra little hop in his step. life was okay. he had to get something to eat. pizza? al taib. uh huh. he got there and ordered a zaatar wrap with cheese instead. all dressed. garlic sauce please. four twenty five. four twenty five? the price went up? yes. man. fine. he walked and ate. he got to the library and just as he finished and tossed the wrapper in the garbage. enter the library. the place was deserted. edgar liked that. he had the entire place to himself, he was the center of the cipher. all those books.

 he set himself up at a table in the middle of the third floor so he could easily be spotted by cal. turned the computer on and flipped through his notes trying to orientate himself. he had sent the bulk of the paper by a friend for feedback. she suggested he strengthen the intro and outro.

linguistic babylon 101: deconstructing 'i & i'

the process of reading this paper will be part of the process of understanding its nature, its reason, or lack thereof. the word *discourse* comes from latin *discurrere*, to run here and there. it has today become whole sets of rigid uses, and i am trying to make it run here and there again.

    yes, you could say this paper has a beginning, a middle and an end, but that's only because we have to start somewhere. it will proceed through a method of simile that can and will keep on going, after this essay, before this essay, and before and after and.

    and is a creative stammering, a foreign language, as opposed to a conformist and dominant use based on the verb "to be". *and* is of course diversity, multiplicity, the destruction of identities, it's not the same factory gate when i go in and come out. it's schizosophical only because it's "foreign" to history, it's unintelligble to it. and i would like to argue that the basis of hip hop culture and other cultures with origins in the african diaspora, such as rastafarianism, are fundamentally schizosophical in regards to the opposing pragmatic reign of babylon that governs society.

i *and* i, '**i & i**', a perfect dualism that represents a relationship between identities....

he got a message from cal. u @ school? ya mahn. c u in a few minutes. word.

❧

cal walked into the library. he used to go all the time, even after he dropped out. he got up to the third floor and found edgar. jesus man, what happened to you? what? do i look that bad? cal's clothes were all dusty, his face was oily, he stunk like cigarettes and the forty he drank the night before, the bottom of his left pant leg was bloodied from the cut he received leaving the fire.

plus he had that glimmer in his eye. that tweaking squeaking of acceleration one gest when strapped into the vortex of limbo.

   he sat down at the table facing edgar. i haven't slept yet. shit man, edgar chuckled, you should go home. i gotta find bobby. did you talk to him today? no. oh...well...how's your paper goin? almost done man, this things been a labour of love, if you can call it that, i guess. you'll let me read it later? i'd want you to read it after. this isn't just some bullshit paper i'm writing so i can have a piece of paper that said i graduated. this is my baby. the seed to the work i will do for the rest of my life. what i want to live and die for. you know what i mean? i do bro, i do. we gotta work together on this shit.

   edgar took out the aluminum wrapped bud and slid it over to cal on the table. thanks man. no problem dude. don't say i never did anything nice for ya. i know you'd do the same. no doubt g. you wanna burn one? i was thinking about it but i want to get this done as soon as i can so i can go outside. okay man, well i'm goin to the tam tams to look for bobby. call him later. ok man. word. thanks again for this. no problem. pounds. see you later. cal strolled out of the library and got suspicious looks from the security guard. he went in the bathroom and looked at himself in the mirror. washed his face, rinsed out his mouth, took a piss and left.

    when he got to the tam tams the mountain side was already littered with people. with frizbees, guitars, soccer balls, footballs, dogs, bikes. there were jugglers, hustlers, dates, mates, hippiers, junkies, funkies in clad. rastas, hipsters, jipsters and tricksters. geeks playing war with swords made of foam from home, cardboard, landboard and etc. posers, loafers and freeloaders. plain clothed cops, pamphleteering talks, can men, clinamen. fuck you thank yous. then, in the center of it all, the magnetic, enigmatic, sonic pragmatic drum circle. surrounded by dancers in trances, eye-tertainment for on lookers, breakers and takers, trumpets and saxomophones. babies and maybe babies that act like young adults and adults that act young like babies and crazies and baby boomers booming boobers with sagging hooters to sharp shooters that are lady soothers of all non-denominational ignorance is bliss kissers from europa to eritria, singapore to the fifth generational from next door, colours like rio and blended so no one will follow but for jokes not for yokes that keep people in scopes with hopes and dreams and fears they might disappear. cal stepped around, behind, in front, through, over. he scanned the masses for a familiar face.

   he stopped in the middle of the park, by the angel statue, and rolled a joint. he smoked and rendered the pixel resolution of his vision. he continued to walk around slowly, stopping by the gazebo, the drum circle, looking around and feeling the sounds. he caught a glimpse of leeloo. he hadn't seen her in a few months. she was beautiful. elegantly plain, one of the most alluring, radical and volatile minds cal had ever met.

   leeloo! she turned around. hiiii she smiled invitingly. she looked happy to see him. hey leeloo, what's up? how you doin? i'm just walking around, it's a nice day. i was supposed to meet a girl and paint but she's not here and her phone is off or something. do you have a phone? no. sorry. i'm having the same problem though. i'm tryin to get a hold of bobby. you know bobby right? you mean that misogynistic epidemic of a snake you call a friend, no i haven't seen him and i don't want to see him.

ah, come on, cal puffed the joint, he's not that bad.   he offered leeloo the joint.   no thanks.
                                                      you're always on drugs.
your always (made.of) drugs (too).

i'm going to go back and see if i can spot my friend. cool, i'll walk with you if you don't mind.   sure.

this friend you're lookin for	this friend that friend
wonder what she looks like	are you guys
supposed to be goin out	on a date or somethin?

                                   i guess so, she giggled.
                                 we've gone out a few times
                                        she's bi

                              but more straight, it's hard to tell.

cal liked to listen to leeloo talk about her experiences with other girls.

she was a male
identified woman
a man
trapped in a   woman's body.
                                          cal respected that.

he used to go to her house . they'd talk for hours.
                    he wanted her. she was a genius.
she once told him that she would only let him fuck her
                    if he was gay

                    they were. are. is.

leeloo didn't believe in the future
the eloi and the morlocks   she swore to disembowel
                                     the genealogy of time

            •she claimed was the biological deficiency of
                                                    humanity
            •she stated that woman wasn't just an invention
                              of intellectual property by man

we used to have two spirits one heart and five genders

   it's interesting you say that because i heard some israelites talking about the defacto principles of the gregorian calender. there'll be a calender more efficient for the second sex, she said. do you think the second sex could be like artaud's psychotic?

      hey, i think i see her! who. maggie. my friend. maggie?

                    really? it was maggie alright,
the same one that cal had met a few weeks ago at the pub.
            you've gotta be kidding me. what? nothing.

no.thing   i know her is all.
                       it looks like she's with bobby and

                                              tina.

and who's that. joe?

they both kept on walking towards the crew who were sitting down in the grass sharing a bottle of wine. what is he doing near her leeloo said defensively. relax, he's with the other girl.

bobby turned his head and noticed
        cal. yo   hey guys.
        calvin kale   ohhhh,
        what's up eh!?   maggie got up and hugged
           both   of   them.

hi guys, i'm so glad to see you. you guys are friends too? cal and leeloo
        looked   at   each other. ya.

        leeloo giggled
            like a little school girl

        cal was weirded right out
                           out right...
    the two sat down and joined.

what happened? i was trying to get a hold of you
                          yo bobby, did you pick up my book bag
hold. aw, sorry, my phone   from your spot? no g. fuck, i forgot it
is dead, i haven't been home yet.   there and went back to find it today
leeloo felt a bit betrayed but smiled   but it was gone. someone must of been
then looked at joe.   there. sorry bro, i didn't see it. what was in
i hadn't heard from you since thursday so it? my notebook, some other books. fuck,
i wasn't sure if you still wanted to meet up. cal was trying not to freak out in front of
                                    everyone, he passed the joint he was
smokin to maggie. oh thanks cal. why did he pass it to her first? she was fucking

joe now? was maggie leading leeloo on or was leeloo trying to convert maggie? cal could tell joe was into maggie but the way joe reacted when cal showed up was maybe a hint that bobby had let joe know that cal was into her and they already had a thing goin on, according to bobby. this whole scene was a bit too much for cal at the time. he didn't care to think about what might be and what might not be. everything just was.

okay. cal got up.

where you goin man? asked bobby.

to rest. i need some quiet time. i'm tired.

word.
bye cal, they said. see y'all sooner than later. word. cal followed his shadow back home, oscillating.

God's Wife and the Synonymous X

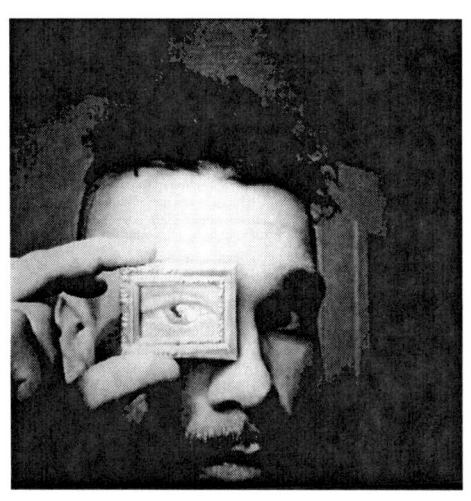

About the Author

JESSE CHASE is a multidisciplinary artist from Montreal. He's published his poetry, interviews, critical theory and reviews in *Poetry is Dead, Arc, Hypermedia Joyce Studies, The Brotherwise Dispatch, The Word Addict* and *Ditch Poetry* magazines. His concrete poetics have been featured in the *Future Concrete Exhibit* in Vancouver and the *Prague Micro Literary Festival*. He also plays trumpet, sings, raps and plays around the city of Montreal regularly.

CPSIA information can be obtained
at www.ICGtesting.com
Printed in the USA
LVOW11s0523271117
557677LV00001B/33/P